RUBE GOLDBERG
AND HIS AMAZING MACHINES

RUBE GOLDBERG

AND HIS AMAZING MACHINES

By Brandon T. Snider

In collaboration with Jennifer George
and the Estate of Rube Goldberg

Illustrated by Ed Steckley

AMULET BOOKS • NEW YORK

Library of Congress Cataloging-in-Publication Data

Names: Snider, Brandon T., writer. | Steckley, Ed, illustrator.
Title: Rube Goldberg and his amazing machines written by Brandon T. Snider ;
illustrated by Ed Steckley.
Description: New York : Amulet Books, [2021] | Audience: Ages 8 to 12
Summary: When on the first day of middle school Principal Kim announces
a Contraption Convention, young inventor Rube Goldberg must conquer his
anxieties and a ghostly mystery to come up with something brilliant for
the judges and his friends.
Identifiers: LCCN 2021017473 | ISBN 9781419750045 (hardcover)
ISBN 9781647000929 (ebook)
Subjects: CYAC: Goldberg, Rube, 1883-1970—Fiction. | Inventions—Fiction.
Middle schools—Fiction. | Schools—Fiction. | Mystery and detective stories.
BISAC: JUVENILE FICTION / Technology / General
JUVENILE FICTION / Mysteries & Detective Stories
Classification: LCC PZ7.S6798 Ru 2021 | DDC [Fic]—dc23
LC record available at https://lccn.loc.gov/2021017473

Text © 2021 Heirs of Rube Goldberg
Illustrations by Ed Steckley
Book design by Brenda E. Angelilli

ABRAMS The Art of Books
195 Broadway, New York, NY 10007
abramsbooks.com

To Jennifer and Rube

CHAPTER 1

"RUUUUUUBE!!!"

The boy's desperate shout cut through the morning calm, sending all the local dogs into a frenzy. He'd been standing outside 7483 Berkeley Street, his best friend's house, for roughly forty seconds. But for an anxious kid like him, that was half a minute too long. It was the first day of school, and if they didn't get their rears in gear, they were going to be late.

"RUBE! C'MON!"

The sun was shining, the birds were chirping, and the morning dew had dried. Once the chill lifted, the heat crept in. A pit had grown in Rube Goldberg's stomach that threatened to swallow him whole. *Nervous* was an understatement. His muscles were tense. There were big changes waiting for him, just around the corner, but he had no idea what they were. He barely got any sleep, tossing and turning for most of the night, obsessed about things that were outside his control. From 4:00 A.M. to 4:30 A.M., he lay in bed worrying about asteroids hitting the planet. From 4:30 A.M. to 5:00 A.M., he stared at the ceiling, irritated by a tiny imperfection no one else noticed but him. It was torturous. But he didn't know what else to do.

"RUBIE!"

Then he put his insomnia to work. It's what he'd been doing all summer anyway. While most kids were swimming in kiddie pools, playing Wiffle ball in their backyards, and otherwise having fun in the sun, Rube was in his bedroom making stuff. He hadn't planned on spending three straight months indoors, that's just how it happened. Back in May, he had high hopes for the summer. The plan was to read up on octopi, learn sign language, plant a banana tree, teach himself how to code, research solar panels, and maybe even install some on his roof. But then something changed. The first week of break, he slept till noon every day. Calls and texts went ignored. Going outside became scary for some strange reason. He couldn't explain it. It felt safer to stay inside, where he could control everything. The broken air conditioner made the whole house hot and stuffy, but Rube didn't care. He had his grandpa's old handkerchief around in case he got too sweaty.

"RUBICON!"

In mid-June, Rube snuck into the attic and rummaged through old boxes. His dad told him not to go up there, because there were

2

"too many wonky nails sticking out of the floor" as well as "questionable spiders." But he did it anyway. When his dad said *not* to do something, all Rube could think about was doing it. Besides, spiders didn't scare him. In the middle of the night, he put on a pair of work boots (wonky nails are no joke, after all) and went looking for stuff. Trinkets? Treasures? He had no idea. He just wanted to build something cool and needed materials to make that happen. There were boxes of ornaments, photographs, strings of lights, and glassware. Typical attic junk. He found his mom's old wedding dress, which had been miraculously preserved among the dust and cobwebs. One weird crate was filled with tools, fishing rods, cymbals, pulleys, doorknobs, wheels, jars, and baby shoes. And a metal helmet with wires sticking out of it that was part of a Halloween costume his dad had made. Among other things. Very quietly, Rube brought down boxes, one after the other, tiptoeing down the hallway so no one would hear him. He poured their contents onto the floor of his room, mixed them together with his own collection of junk, and created a monster pile of stuff. At first, he wasn't sure what to do with any of it. But then his mind's wheels started turning.

"RHUBARB! RUBILICIOUS!"

While downing an ice-cold glass of lemonade one steamy July afternoon, Rube remembered something. His grandma had given him a fancy Italian notebook she bought while on vacation with her old-lady dance team, the Movers and Shakers. He'd stuffed it into a drawer and forgotten about it. But when ideas started percolating inside his head, Rube drew them. Sometimes he'd doodle comic strips. Other times, he'd design simple machines, gadgets, and dream inventions. Over time, the notebook's fake leather binding frayed around the edges. It smelled like grape soda, but that was only because Rube had spilled grape soda all over it, then let it sit in a hot car for a week. His mom once told him to write down his thoughts if he ever felt overwhelmed or frustrated. "Get them out of that noggin and onto the page," she said. "That way, they won't make you sick." He wished he would've listened.

"REUBEN GARRETT LUCIUS GOLDBERG!"

The kid standing on Rube's lawn, screaming like a maniac, was his best friend, Boob McNutt. Rube and Boob were more than just friends. Brothers? Soul mates? They didn't put a label on it. Rube had Boob's back. Boob had Rube's back. That's all that mattered. Sure, they argued on occasion, but they always made up over a bowl of mochi. That is, unless Rube had a stash of international snacks his dad bought during his travels. Over the years, they'd started no fewer than five different clubs where *they* were the only members. Toy Club was fun until Boob accidentally ate a Lego and had to go to the hospital. Don't ask how they got the Lego out.

4

Sports Club fell apart quickly once they realized neither of them cared about sports. Technically, Nature Club was still around, but it only really mattered whenever they found a weird insect or a peculiar piece of wood. As for the other two clubs, they don't even remember. Rube and Boob moved fast and were always into something new . . . until they weren't. It's just how they rolled.

Oh, and Boob knows you think his name is weird. He just doesn't care.

"RUUUUUUUBE!" Boob screamed. He was at his wit's end. **"GET YOUR BUTT DOWN HERE RIGHT NOW!"**

Rube poked his face out the window of his second-floor bedroom. "What?" he asked calmly.

"Stop messing around. We have to go!"

"Can't. I'm working on a thing."

"We're going to be late!"

"Not if we run."

"Don't joke like that. Dr. Lipschitz said my kneecaps are the size of pebbles. If I

run, my legs will fall apart like twigs."

"No, they won't. You're making that up."

"They might! You don't know. The human body is a very complicated machine. Plus, I'm already sweating so much. If we run, I'll be drenched by the time we get there. Drenched! On the first day of middle school! It's not a good look."

"We're going to have to start using deodorant soon, aren't we? Ugh."

"You have no idea what I've had to deal with today. First, I woke up super late, then I got grape jelly all over my favorite shirt, then my bike was stolen."

"Not my problem. Wait. Your bike was stolen?"

"Rube, why are you being like this? Let's go!"

"I'm working on something very cool. I'm in the zone. My juices are flowing. I can't abandon ship now. Not even for school."

"Is this that Fold-Up Toilet you told me about? No one will buy that thing. Trust me. My dad spends *at least* two hours on the toilet every single day, and even *he* said it was a bad idea."

"Think bigger."

"Cupcake Cannon?"

"Nah."

"Butter Slide?"

"Nope. But I like where you're going with this . . ."

"Ugh, I give up. Can you please just put some pants on and get down here?!"

"How'd you know I wasn't wearing pants? You can't see my lower half."

"Duh. I've known you since you were five years old."

"Good call. Nice to see *you* dressed up for this special occasion."

"Ha," Boob said with a flat stare. His style was all about comfort: a simple shirt coupled with a pair of pajama bottoms. It was his uniform, no matter the season. Boob loved a bold print, and today's selection was extra special. "These are my lucky night pants."

"It's daytime. And you say that about every pair you own. How'd your mom even let you out of the house in those monstrosities?"

"She was sleeping when I left. Come on! I have to pee soon, and I'd prefer to do it in a bathroom."

Rube looked down at his faithful sidekick, Bertha, who was doing her two favorite things—licking her lips and panting. She was a *dog*, after all. "The lady of the house says hello."

"Hey, Bertha. Now quit stalling!"

Queen Bertha was a rescue with no backstory. She was abandoned in a parking lot and adopted by Rube's family a week later. They called her their "hairy little hodgepodge," since her breed was

8

a total mystery. Bertha adored Rube and loved being by his side. She snuggled him through good times, bad times, weird times, and crazy times. Bertha also loved to venture out of the house when no one was looking. Everyone in town knew her, and not just because she did her business anywhere she wanted (her favorite place to poop was in front of the courthouse). Her personality was legendary. Bertha was smarter than most dogs, with a very keen sense of people. If she didn't like you, you might actually be a bad guy. Then again, Bertha also chased her tail, growled at her butt, and ate gravel. Her senses weren't 100 percent right all the time.

"I just need one more minute," Rube said, shutting the window. His creation was almost complete. All it needed were a few final touches. He'd begun sketching the thing around 6:00 A.M., finishing around 6:30 A.M. By 7:00 A.M., he'd corralled all the necessary materials. At 7:30 A.M., he was ready to go. But then he stopped himself. His brain told him his idea wouldn't work. *Pack it in, Goldberg. You'll just fail anyway. Do you really think this will work? You're twelve years old! You don't know squat about squat. Everyone will laugh at you. Your dad will probably kick you out of the house. Life as you know it will come crashing down. You sure you want to risk it?* Eventually, Rube realized his brain was just being a jerk. He shook out of his stupor and got his head in the game. It was time to test his new creation, the *Sprucer-Upper*, a

machine that would revolutionize room cleaning and change the world! *Maybe*. With his hand shaking just a little bit, Rube set the machine in motion. Things went well for a couple seconds . . . until Bertha intervened. She jumped onto the Sprucer-Upper and spun around like an out-of-control top. Parts flew in every direction as she whipped her backside all over the place. When the commotion ended, the machine was in shambles, reduced to the pile of junk from which it sprang. Rube sat on the floor of his room, defeated. Bertha sensed her master's disappointment and happily licked his face to make it all better. "Thanks, girl?"

Outside on the curb, Boob had attracted unwanted attention with his cries. "Oh no," he muttered. A police car pulled up, and a lanky officer with wild limbs and a bushy mustache hopped out. As he made a beeline toward Boob, his noodle arms flipped and flapped all over the place.

"What's going on here? We got a report of a pervert in the area, screaming about"—the officer pursed his lips—"*rear ends.*"

"That was me!" Boob said with a burst of bountiful exuberance. Then he thought for a moment. "Um, what I meant to say was, *I* was the one screaming about butts. I mean, uh, my friend's butt. Because he's not moving it. But I'm not a . . ." He flailed his arms to clear the air. "Let me start over."

"Bullet points, kid," said the officer. "I don't have time for tom-toolery."

"Who has time for *anything* these days, am I right?" The scowl on the officer's face told Boob he needed to get to the point ASAP. "My friend doesn't want to go to school. He says he's 'working on something,' but it's our first day of middle school and I think he's just nervous."

"I'M NOT NERVOUS!" Rube shouted from inside the house.

The police officer reached into his cruiser and pulled out a bullhorn. "I need you to step back, son," he said, cracking his neck. "What's this boy's name?"

"Rube. But his full name is Reuben. Like the sandwich."

"And what's *your* name?"

"Boob."

The officer did a double take. "*Boob*? Like the . . . ?"

"*Nope.* And you are"—he squinted at the officer's badge—"*Officer Bacon.*" Boob desperately wanted to oink like a little piggy, but he also didn't want to start any more trouble. So he nodded kindly. "As in . . . ?"

"Sir Francis Bacon, who invented the scientific method that says . . ." He stopped himself from explaining further. "Now is not the time. I have work to do." He raised the bullhorn to his mouth and let loose. "RUBE, THIS IS OFFICER BACON OF THE BEECH-WOOD POLICE DEPARTMENT. YOU ARE TO EXIT YOUR HOME WITH YOUR BACKPACK AND MAKE YOUR WAY TO SCHOOL IMMEDIATELY. FAILURE TO COMPLY WILL RESULT IN A TRUANCY REPORT."

Boob looked at his watch. "We'll need a ride too, while you're at it."

The front door opened and out walked Rube, backpack over his shoulder and notebook in his hand. He stopped on the sidewalk and took one last look at the sanctuary he was leaving behind *There's no going back. This is happening.* "What's everyone standing around for? C'mon. We're gonna be late."

Officer Bacon opened the car door, ushering the boys into the back seat like a chauffeur.

"To Beechwood Middle School!" Boob cheered. "And make it snappy."

The first few minutes of the ride were silent and awkward, until Officer Bacon broke the ice. "So . . ." The tiny word lingered in the air, making the boys nervous. Rube looked at Boob. Boob looked at Rube. They each knew exactly what the other one was thinking. *We've been kidnapped, and neither of us ever took the time to learn jujitsu!* Before they had a chance to beg for their lives, Officer Bacon finished his sentence. "How was your summer?"

"I don't have to answer your questions, Copper!" Boob always had an uncontrollable response on standby.

"Please excuse my friend, Officer," Rube said. "He's a little excitable."

Boob took a deep breath and relaxed into his seat as if he owned the car. "My summer was good, actually. Except for getting sunburned at the pool and puking in the deep end. They closed the pool for good after that. Not because of me, because it ran out of money. I think. Then I went to the library to get started on my Summer Reading List but forgot which books I was supposed to get, so I checked out one about the history of Beechwood and, guys, I don't know if you know this, but our town is full of secrets. Dark, unspoken secrets."

"How are they unspoken if you read about them?"

"Shhhh. You'll attract evil spirits. This place is riddled with ghosts."

"There's no such thing as ghosts."

"Rueben! Yes. There. Is. Ancient druids from faraway lands settled here and cursed our town. That's why I have this." Boob pulled his shirt collar down to reveal a purple crystal pendant. "Cool, right? Went to a gem and mineral show when my family was on vacation. Hoping it protects me from specters. New year, new me!"

"You say that every year."

"Yeah, because I'm evolving!" Boob said. "Anyway, we should be extra careful because Beechwood is seriously cursed."

"What about you?" Officer Bacon asked. He shot Rube a steely glare in the rearview mirror. "What did *you* get up to this summer?"

Rube wasn't in the mood to talk. His stomach was in knots. All he could think about was walking into school and having everyone make fun of him. For what? He had no idea. He just assumed everyone would. "Slept. Ate hot dogs. Made stuff. Watched Godzilla movies."

"*Godzilla vs. Mechagodzilla* is best!" Boob exclaimed.

"*So good*. Probably my favorite. I could watch it forever."

"What kind of stuff do you make?" asked Officer Bacon.

"He likes to build robots out of junk."

"Not *junk*. Not *robots*," Rube insisted. "*Machines*."

"You should make one for the Science Fair."

Rube's ears perked up. *A spark of hope.* He almost forgot about the Science Fair.

"So, you're a *builder*?" asked Officer Bacon. "Is that it?"

"I guess." Rube shrugged.

As the police cruiser turned a corner, it passed by one of the town's most notorious homes. A place *you did not go*. It was surrounded by a rickety old fence and nestled comfortably at the top of a steep hill. The local kids called it the Haunted Hideaway. Accidentally toss a football into the yard? Say goodbye, because it's not coming back. On the outside, the house looked abandoned.

There were rumors around town that it belonged to a reclusive older gentleman. A mad-scientist type who rarely went outside and who no one knew much about. Some said he did his gardening in the dead of night. *Naked.* Neighborhood kids etched the name Lucifer on his mailbox. No one could confirm the place was actually haunted, but its dark windows definitely gave it a spooky vibe. The townspeople wanted it torn down, but since the house was so old, it had been declared a historic landmark. That meant no one could do much of anything except complain. Rube's father told him to stay away, so he did. But he never stopped being curious. The place was surrounded by all kinds of trash and other rusty junk. A tetanus shot waiting to happen. All Rube saw were *treasures.* Beautiful machine parts waiting for a good home. As he pressed his face against the car window, one particular piece caught his eye—a collapsible accordion rack. It was totally old-school (his favorite kind of school) and perfect for some of the machines he'd been thinking about. *I absolutely gotta get my hands on that.*

In the rearview mirror, Officer Bacon noticed Rube staring. "Don't even think about it," he said, waving his finger.

"The Haunted Hideaway was in my book," Boob mumbled. "My mom said the owner grows something called *wacky tuhbacky*. Whatever that is. I wonder if *he's* a druid."

"Look, I gotta ask . . ." Office Bacon began. Boob knew exactly what was coming next. *The most annoying question in the world.* "How'd you get such a weird name?"

Having told his origin story a thousand times over the course of his life, Boob was officially sick of it. Of course, he couldn't say that to Officer Bacon. Unless he was looking for trouble. Which he wasn't. Sometimes he'd outright lie because it sounded much more exciting than the truth. *I'm the secret grandson of His Royal Highness King Boobalon the Second, spirited away in the night to live a normal life in small-town America, a far cry from the hubbub of his former island kingdom.* The boring truth was that his birth name was Bob. Just Bob. But his weird older brother, who had an un-

definable speech impediment, pronounced Bob as Boob way back when they were babies. The name stuck. The rest is history. It wasn't until Boob got older that he understood why people laughed at him. But by then it didn't matter.

"*Luck*," Boob said with a cheeky smile.

"Why don't you change it?" asked Officer Bacon.

Rube was irked by the line of questioning. "Because he shouldn't have to change something about himself just to make other people comfortable. Drop it."

Boob poked Rube in his side. "You can't say that to an officer of the law," he whispered. "We'll end up in a gulag."

"You don't even know what a gulag is," Rube replied. He scrunched up his face and looked out the window. Someone was getting testy.

Boob leaned over, giving Rube a closer look. "Oh wow. Your baby mustache is coming in really nicely."

Rube rubbed his upper lip, feeling the thin coating of fuzz. "Talk about something else, please." His anxious hand tightened around his notebook.

"Can I see that?" Boob asked. "I wanna look at your machine thingies." As he tried to grab the notebook, Rube crammed the thing into his backpack and zipped it shut.

"Maybe later."

It wasn't like Rube not to give his best friend an all-access pass to his stuff. But this was different. Everyone knew Rube dabbled in various things, but he hadn't shared his passion for machines with *anyone*. In his mind, no one else could possibly understand the things he wanted to build. They were too complicated. *Or silly.* He couldn't decide. For the moment, they were his and his alone.

Rube just didn't feel like explaining.

All of a sudden, Boob's face began contorting into strange shapes. *Oh no. He's going to cry, isn't he?* His nose twitched. His eyes blinked rapidly. *Wait. He's not going to cry, he's going to*—"AHHHHH-CHOO!" Boob sneezed into his arm, leaving behind a patch of yellow goo.

"Snot arm!" Rube exclaimed, pointing.

"Don't hassle me. I've got allergies," Boob said, shoving it in Rube's face. "See."

"Get it away from me, Boob! I'm serious."

"Hey!" snapped Officer Bacon. "You two cut it out back there."

"What will you do if we don't? Arrest us?" Rube whispered to himself.

Boob pulled a tissue out of his pocket and wiped away the snot glop. "It's too hot in here," he whined. "Can you roll down the window or something?"

"No," said Officer Bacon. He still couldn't get over the name. "*Boob.* That's friggin' hysterical. Do you know how crazy that is?"

Rube rolled his eyes so hard they almost made a sound. "No, he doesn't know how crazy that is. *You*, Officer Bacon, are the first person to ever point this out. And now that I'm seeing it? Wow. *So friggin' hysterical.* How lucky we are to have someone so enlightened protecting our town from danger. Our tax dollars at work!"

Officer Bacon's tone changed. "Oh, so you wanna be a smart-guy, huh?"

"I *am* a smart guy," Rube countered.

Boob elbowed him gently. "*Don't get us arrested*. I'm not dressed for a mug shot. And what do *you* know about tax dollars?"

"Nothing," Rube replied. "I just heard that on the news."

"You seemed like good kids," Officer Bacon said, shaking his head in disbelief. "But I can see now you're just a couple of wisenheimers."

"I'm not just any old wisenheimer, sir. I'm an official member of the Wisenheimer Society," said Rube. "My *father* was a wisenheimer. *His* father was a wisenheimer. My *dog* is a wisenheimer. It's a family affair."

"*I* actually come from a long line of *Johnny Jokesters*," Boob countered.

"Heh," Officer Bacon scoffed.

Buy a sense of humor, dude.

"Comedically speaking, we're unstoppable," Boob whispered to Rube. "Remember back when we were little and used to put on variety shows for our stuffed animals? We should do that again. But with people."

"*Two* of your teddy bears got up and left the room when I sang 'Bohemian Rhapsody.' I think I'm done performing for a while."

"Whoa! I forgot about that. The batteries in th___ were running out of juice. When that happens, they ten___ mind of their own (it's kind of scary). Don't take it personai, Your rendition of 'Bohemian Rhapsody' was *stellar*."

"Thanks, buddy. Your version of 'Can You Feel the Love To-night' is pretty great too. Hits me in the feels every time," Rube said, pretending to get choked up.

The sounds of chaos grew louder as they approached Beech-wood Middle School. The closer they got, the more anxious Rube became. He squirmed in his seat, massaged his neck, and clutched his stomach. Something was wrong. "Ahem, ahem, AHEM," he coughed.

"What's the matter?" Boob asked. "Sounds like your throat is closing up."

"That's because my throat is closing up."

"Oo-oo-oo, I should be a doctor." Boob wiggled his eyebrows. "Don't sweat it, Rube. My dad said middle school was the best worst time of his life."

"That means it was *bad*, Boob."

"No, it doesn't. He said it was the best . . ." Boob did the math. "Oh no. No, no, no. I've made a terrible mistake. Take us home. Please, Officer, take us home!"

Officer Bacon pulled into the drop-off area behind a long line minivans and put the car in park. "Look, kids, I get it. You're scared. Everything is new." He turned around, placing his arm on the headrest. "Your bodies are going through changes."

"MEOW, MEOW, MEOW, MEOW, MEOW," Boob screeched, stuffing his fingers into his ears. Whenever he wanted something (or someone) to go away, he'd make animal noises till they couldn't stand it anymore. It didn't always do the trick.

"That's enough!" shouted Officer Bacon. "All I'm saying is, everything is going to be fine. Middle school isn't the end of the world."

Based on what Rube saw out the window of the police cruiser, he was doubtful. Kids pushed and shoved their way through the schoolyard as they headed for the school's front doors. Old classmates, new classmates, and everyone in between came twisting in from all directions like ants marching into an overstuffed colony. The chaos had left the poor bike rack looking like a disaster area. Rube's eyes darted across the crowd, searching for someone he couldn't quite find. Some people had physically changed so much over the summer that it was hard to tell who was who. Puberty hit some of them like a brick, while others waited patiently for it to kick in. Short kids who'd suffered at the hands of bullies had miraculously grown tall. Tall kids, once known for their sparkling complexion, now had pimples. And the pimpled kids? They trans-

formed into beautiful butterflies. Middle school was officially the United Nations of hormones. It was impressive and frightening.

"Look, you want to know the best advice I can give you? Act normal. That way, you won't attract any trouble." Officer Bacon exited the vehicle and opened the door for his guests.

"We appreciate the ride, Officer." Boob reached into his pocket, pulled out a dollar bill, and handed it to Officer Bacon. "Get yourself something nice."

Officer Bacon furrowed his brow and pushed the bill away. "Don't, kid." With a tip of his cap, he got in his car and peeled off.

"Screw normal," Rube said.

Out of nowhere, a pair of familiar and unwelcoming faces were coming in hot. Mike and Ike were known as the Jockensteins, a little bit jock and a little bit Frankenstein. That's what Boob called them behind their back. Lumbering zombies who were also reasonably good on the football field. As identical twins, Mike and Ike messed with everyone around them—their parents, their siblings, their classmates, their teachers. Even the lunch ladies. Switching places always made it easy for them to shift blame. "It wasn't me!" was practically their catchphrase. But now that they were getting older and becoming individuals, it wasn't as easy to hide anymore.

Mike and Ike never went anywhere without their cell phones. They got a kick out of shoving them in people's faces. Mike aimed

his phone at Rube and pressed record. "A police escort!?" he shouted. "What'd you do, Goldberg? Mug a guy?"

"Yeah, Mike. Keep your distance," Rube said. His tone was so dry it was crispy. "I'm a dangerous weapon. You don't want none, there won't be none."

"Hey, Boobie," Ike said, shifting his focus and thrusting his phone at Boob. "How are your *boobies*? Hahaha!"

Boob tilted his head and grinned directly into the camera. Not because he thought Ike was funny but rather, he knew this moment was coming. Mike and Ike were predictable creatures. Boneheads to the core. And Boob was ready to dismantle them. "You mean to tell me you had *all summer* to come up with brand-new material

and *that's* what you went with?"

Ike didn't understand the dig. "Uhhhh, what?"

"You could've said, 'I guess Goldberg hit puberty over the summer, because his *Boob* looks a lot bigger,' or 'Here comes Rube and Boob, a couple of *bosom buddies.*' Those are *clever*! Those are *funny*! What you said was lame and, frankly, sad."

"Whatever," Ike scoffed. "Shut up."

"Awwwww. You mad 'cuz you got"—Boob paused for dramatic effect—"*busted*?"

Rube chuckled.

"You think he's funny?" asked Mike.

"Of course I do," Rube replied. "He's my *breast* friend."

"See! What *we're* doing is comedy. What *you're* doing is stupid. Everything you've ever said and will ever say to me? It's been said a thousand times before. So until you come up with something new and original, keep your grimy mouthhole shut," Boob said firmly. "Thanks."

Mike and Ike weren't used to being put in their place like that. It made them mad but also confused them (though neither was all that bright to begin with). They looked at each other square in the eyes, as if sending and receiving angry telepathic messages. Defeated, they put their phones in their pockets and walked away. "This ain't over," Mike mumbled to himself.

"Hey! One more thing," Boob shouted. Mike and Ike turned around. "Thanks for helping me get that off my chest."

Rube put his arm around Boob. "My friend, you are truly *one in a melon*."

Suddenly, everyone's attention shifted. A black stretch limo pulled up to the curb and a sea of photographers swarmed the area, descending from the trees in the nearby park. They'd been patiently waiting since before sunrise. Many of them flew in from New York City and Los Angeles just to get a single shot. Lala Palooza, Beechwood Middle School's most famous student, had finally appeared. And not a moment too soon.

Lala's chauffeur, Hives, opened the car door and presented her

to the world. Extending her leg in a dramatic fashion, Lala daintily stepped out and struck a pose. Ever the professional, Lala put her hand on her hip, threw her head back, and pretended to laugh as a flurry of flashbulbs started snapping. Months ago, her team of stylists had pored over hundreds of combinations to come up with the perfect first-day-of-school outfit. An oversize sweatshirt, vintage skinny jeans, and a pair of fresh kicks. No makeup. Lala was always au naturel. The look was effortlessly casual, except for the diamond barrettes on loan from a fancy European jeweler. Everyone in the schoolyard was mesmerized. Students, teachers, parents. Even the squirrels were doing double takes.

"Regardez-vous tous, salivant comme une meute de loups affamés. Animaux. Chacun d'eux. Vous me dégoutez! Pourtant, je joue ici le rôle de la petite fille heureuse que vous voulez tous que je sois. Un jour bientôt, tout changera. Vous verrez,"[1] Lala said with passion, outrageous fluency, and vigor. Despite her Latin American roots, French was actually Lala's favorite language. It made her feel like an international superspy. She also loved the fact that most people had no idea what she was saying. "You've got thirty

---

1 French translation: "Look at all of you, salivating like a pack of starving wolves. Animals. Each of you. You disgust me! Yet here I play the role of the happy girl that you all want me to be. One day soon, everything will change. You will see."

seconds to get your shots. K?"

When Lala's famous parents settled in Beechwood, the community was a little confused. Why would a celebrity family put down roots in a Podunk suburb? It was a mystery no one could figure out, especially considering that Lala's parents were rarely in town. Most of the time, they were either vacationing or on location shooting a movie. That left Lala home alone to do whatever she pleased. After a disastrous stint at a French boarding school, she was exiled to public school, where things were a little less easy for her, despite the fame. The mean girls wanted her to lead them, but she wasn't interested. She didn't go to their parties or follow their style. Lala did her own thing, and they ended up despising her for it. When she first arrived in town, Rube was the only person who had the guts to talk to her like a normal person. She never forgot that.

"All right, that's it, we're done," Lala said, giving the paparazzi a final twirl. As the photographers began packing up, one troll-looking man stood out among them. He kept snapping photos, one after the other, getting closer and closer to Lala in the process. "You're done, sir." She waved him away like a dog begging for scraps. "Pack it up. Show some respect." The man kept snapping . . . which left Lala with no choice but to retaliate. She swung the car door open to reveal two yellow eyes. They glowed brightly inside a dark corner of the limousine. "Rolex hasn't eaten yet. Wanna feed him?" The sound of hissing grew louder as Lala's cat stepped forward. *MEOWCH!* Rolex swiped his claws, frightening the trollish photographer, who jumped back, tripped over himself, and fell to the ground. Fumbling, he picked up his camera and ran away. "Bye-eee." Lala kissed Rolex on the forehead and headed inside the school. But not before catching the eye of a friend. "Hey, Rube," she said, beaming. "Let's catch up soon."

While he didn't *exactly* have a crush on Lala, Rube definitely thought she was cute. Instead of saying "hello" back like a normal person, he responded with a peace sign that morphed into a two-handed wave. Confused by the odd gesture, Lala just kept walking.

"I heard if the seventh-grade boys don't like you, they'll steal your regular clothes during gym, then burn them," Boob said. "I just hope the bathroom stalls have doors."

BRRRRRRRRRING!

"Ooops. Gotta go. Check ya later!" Boob had a bad habit of shuffling his feet when he walked, which often caused his shoelaces to become entangled. As he picked up the pace, his messy laces tripped him up, causing him to smack the pavement with a *THUD*. "I'm okay! I'm okay!" he said to no one in particular. After carefully sorting himself out, Boob jogged up the steps to safety.

Rube took a good, long look at his new school. From the outside, the place where he'd be spending the next three years of his life didn't look so hot. *Outdated, to be exact.* But his choices were limited. There was nothing he could do but accept his fate. While students rushed inside, Rube scanned the crowd again but still didn't find who he was looking for.

SWACK! In the rush of students, a tall boy with black hair unexpectedly slammed into Rube's back, sending books flying in all directions. "Sorry," the boy said. His long, dark bangs fell over his face, hiding his eyes. Rube reached down to help him pick up his books but was waved away. "Don't worry about it." The boy quickly gathered his things and darted into the building.

BRRRRRRRRRING!

"First day of sixth grade," Rube said flatly. "Let's get this over with."

CHAPTER 2

Light-years from Earth, on the glistening bridge of the starship *Minerva*, a bearded man in a white tunic looked out across the universe and was pleased. He'd been waiting a long time for this moment. Now that he had accomplished his goal, he felt complete. And maybe a little hungry. Behind him, the ship's crew busied themselves, pressing buttons and gazing at computer screens.

"We've done it, Great Creator," said one of the ship's officers. "We've found a way back home to Earth. And it's all because of *you*."

The bearded man took a seat at the helm of the ship. He closed his eyes and savored the moment. At once, he was finally at ease. The struggle had ended. Now a new path was on the horizon. His stomach growled ferociously. "Excuse me."

"*Rube* . . ." A small, hooded figure in a crimson cloak whispered from the back of the control room. "*You don't know what you're doing.*"

The bearded man turned in surprise. Only *he* could see the hooded figure. "Who are you?" he asked, his body filling with fear. "How do you know my name?"

"You *know* who I am," the figure growled.

"Are you . . . *Death*?"

The figure whipped off his hood. "Do I *look* like Death to you?" It was Rube himself. The kid version. "What a drama queen. You really love to make things difficult for yourself, don't you? *Dummy*. Nice beard, Grandpa. How old are you? Forty!?" He strolled across the deck of the ship, inspecting each and every little thing.

"What do you want with me?" asked Old Rube.

Kid Rube cackled. "Hahahaha! *Nothing.* I'm just giving you a hard time. It's my job. *Our* job, really. Unless something changes. Which it won't. You got any snacks around here?" He opened a cabinet and found it bare. "Ugh. What a waste of time."

"Tell me why you've come here!" Old Rube demanded. "*What is your purpose?*"

"Guess we'll find out, won't we? Now *wake up.* You're slobbering all over the place."

The bright starship faded to black. When Rube awoke in reality, he found himself in the middle of class. "*GAH!*" he shouted, jerking his head up from the sweat-covered desk. A dribble of drool dripped from the corner of his mouth. It cascaded down his chin, en route to his neck. As soon as he felt it, he wiped the droplet away and pretended everything was fine.

"What do you think, Mr. Goldberg?" asked his teacher, Ms. Shankar.

Rube was discombobulated and unsure of his surroundings. Dozing off in class will do that to you. Everyone in the room was fixed on what Rube would do next. Glancing down at the social studies book on his desk, he searched his brain for something, *anything*, that sounded even the slightest bit useful. A fun fact, a tidbit, a morsel? Rube had nothing. Then he remembered when his family went on a trip to visit the National Museum of the American

Indian in New York City. He'd bought a book in the gift shop. Memorized it in a week. *I've got just the thing.*

"Um, well, you know, this reminds me of Cherokee mythology. There were these immortal spirits, kind of like fairies, called the Nunnehi. They were born from dreams and lived inside human bodies. Their name means 'the people who live anywhere.' Cool, right?" Rube glanced around the room, searching for faces of approval, but there were none. Only looks of confusion and a few giggles. Ms. Shankar seemed humored at best.

"*Wow.* What an interesting response," she said. "Thank you for that, Rube."

"No problem," Rube said, breathing a sigh of relief. "*Anytime.*"

"But this is algebra class." Ms. Shankar pointed to a poster in the corner that said ALGEBRA IS FUN, with the words surrounded by party hats and colorful balloons.

A wave of embarrassment swept across Rube's body. He wanted to hide under his desk, shrink to the size of a flea, and disappear completely. Thankfully, a diversion arrived in a surprise announcement blasting through the crackling intercom.

"All students, please report to the gym for an assembly. All students, please report to the gym for an assembly. Thank you."

Ms. Shankar nodded at the teacher's aide, Mr. Ogle, a fashionable young man with a mustache and dark glasses. "Single-file line," he said, ushering the students out of the room.

"No homework tonight. But be prepared for a pop quiz later this week," said Ms. Shankar. "Rube, hang back for a second."

Rube lingered in the doorway, books in hand, waiting patiently for his punishment. He'd heard mixed reviews on Ms. Shankar. Some kids thought she was "cool" (because she was in her mid-twenties and went to concerts), while others said she "wasn't terrible" (because she still gave homework).

But the lady had undeniable style and grace. Her cardigan was impeccable, and her skirt was neatly pressed. Though her hair was known to become frizzier as the day went on.

"I know algebra can be boring, but falling asleep in class on the first day of school is *harsh*. Was it my lack of funny voices and silly songs? I wrote a rap about factoring quadratics, if you want to hear it."

"Uh, no, thanks."

"That's probably for the best," said Ms. Shankar. "My eighth-grade class told me I don't have *bars*, which would probably hurt my feelings if I knew what it meant."

"It means you can't rap."

"Oh. How unfortunate." There was disappointment in Ms. Shankar's voice. "I'll have to work on that. Anyway, what's up with sleeping in class?"

Well, you see, I don't want to be here. The raw truth was too much for Ms. Shankar to handle, so he went with a modified version.

"I was up late. And up early. A little bit of both."

Ms. Shankar knew the feeling. "It's difficult to adjust to a new routine after a whole summer of sleeping in every day, eating junk food, and watching trashy reality shows like *Omelet Wars* and *Renovate My Cousin*. But enough about me. Let's talk about you. What are you looking forward to this year, Rube?"

"The Science Fair sounds cool."

"You know, science and math go hand in hand . . ."

Rube stayed silent. He *really* didn't want to do this right now.

Ms. Shankar could tell. She took off her glasses, laid them on her desk, and got serious. "Rube, things are changing for you, academically speaking. It's important to stay on the right track. That means studying and having an eye toward making good grades. If you're having trouble focusing, there are ways to help you. It wouldn't hurt to stop by the guidance counselor's office."

I hate this, I hate this, I hate this. "May I go now? I don't want to miss the assembly."

"You can, but first you have to answer my riddle. Do you know why plants hate math?"

This is too easy. "Because it gives them *square roots.*"

Ms. Shankar was impressed. "Get out of here," she said, waving him away. "And don't forget to study for that pop quiz!"

Rube took his sweet time getting to the assembly. He peeked his head into the Art Room, enjoyed a quick squirt at the drinking fountain, and strolled down the windowed corridor. The scent of fresh pizza bagels was already drifting through the halls. Beechwood Middle looked fairly normal on the outside and had all the typical stuff. A playground, a flagpole, and a sign out front that said WELCOME STUDENTS! in big letters. No one really thought of the place as unremarkable, but it was. A pipe had burst years ago, flooding a bunch of classrooms, but instead of building new ones, they just doubled up. The classes got larger as the spaces got smaller. The carpets were so dingy and stained they just layered other carpets on top to hide any undesirable spots. Teachers tried to speak up, but the district superintendent told them to keep quiet or they'd lose their jobs. The school color scheme of pea green and pumpkin orange was painfully out-of-date. Kids said it reminded them of being forced to eat their vegetables. Everyone did their best with what they had, but it was clear to anyone with two eyes and a brain that Beechwood Middle School was in desperate need of a makeover.

Rube was surprised to see a familiar face welcoming the students into the assembly. "Mr. Kim?!" he exclaimed. "What are you doing here?"

"It's *Principal* Kim now," said the short man in spectacles and an ill-fitting brown suit. His clothes looked to be about two sizes too small for his frame. It was as if he'd been blasted by a wonky shrinking ray that only shrunk his body. "C'mon, Rube. Get in there and take a seat." Theodore Kim used to be the security officer at Beechwood Elementary. Before that, he was the school's janitor. Before *that*, he was an assistant manager at Taco Cavern. Now, somehow, he'd become the principal of Beechwood Middle and the person in charge of the next three years of Rube's academic life. *This is not good.*

Inside the gym, Rube was slapped in the face by his new reality. There were sixth, seventh, and eighth graders crawling all over one another. It was loud. *Crazy* loud. Some kids were screaming for no reason. A group of seventh-grade boys had unleashed a bunch of toads. One of the science teachers, Mrs. Poloski, scooped them up and bundled them in her skirt so they wouldn't escape. Nothing made sense. Last year, Rube knew every single one of his class-mates. Now there were twice as many. *Where will I sit?* He spotted a familiar face in "Jungle" Jimmy Reynolds, who once peed his pants on purpose while hanging upside down on the jungle gym back in second grade. Next to him was Hayley Gunter. She always had a broken leg for some reason. One time, Rube saw her take her cast off and ride her bike home. He never told anyone about it.

"Rube!" Boob shouted, waving his arms like a wild child. "Over here!" He was sitting between Jayden Jacobs and Addison Riley, who were in their fourth year as sixth graders. No one knew why, though. They weren't failing their classes or anything. There was a rumor floating around that they were actually adults in disguise, working undercover. No one believed it. *Mostly.* Rube pushed his way through the row and wedged himself next to his best friend.

"How's your day going?" asked Boob.

"Meh," Rube replied.

"I hear ya," said Boob. "It's been a mixed bag so far for me too. But I found a cool book in the library," Boob added, showing off the hardcover volume. "More local legends. Did you know there's a secret cemetery in the woods? We should find it. Oh, and there's

this little girl named Gladys who died in a fire. I think. Or she was eaten by wolves. Whatever, I still need to read the book. Anyway, people said her restless spirit has been known to haunt—"

"Nice kicks, McNutt." Jayden pushed his shoulder into Boob's. "Find 'em in the creek?"

Boob's sneakers were old and worn, their laces frayed. Money was tight, and his dad refused to get him new ones. "Yeah, I did, Jayden. They were right behind *your mom's* house."

Jayden's hands quickly formed fists. "Don't, Jay," Addison said. "This kid is nothing." The duo moved to another row, but Boob couldn't resist rubbing salt in Jayden's wounds.

"I'd call your mom a swamp witch, but I've met her before and she's actually a really nice lady. Don't know how she ended up with such a donkey dimple for a son."

Rube raised his brow. "A what?"

"I'm trying out alternative curse words. Hopefully, they'll catch on," Boob replied. "Did you see *Mr. Kim* is now our principal?! He's about to make a big announcement that the government wants to add more days to the school year. Summers would only be a month, and we'd have class on Christmas Day."

"That's not true."

"Yes, it is! My dad said a guy at the gas station told him. This guy knows what he's talking about too, since he used to work for the CBD."

"You mean the CIA."

"Whatever. Just wait. *School. On Christmas.* You'll see."

Rube stopped listening to Boob's rambling to focus on something else. There was still someone he needed to locate. He craned his head, eyes searching in every direction, but he hadn't found them yet.

Principal Kim's jittery assistant, Miss Mary, entered the gym carrying an overstuffed box of T-shirts. She was an average sort of woman except for the strange way she applied her makeup. Earlier in the day, Rube caught Miss Mary looking at her reflection in the school trophy cases. She was making nutty faces, one after the other. First a smile, then a frown, then she pursed her lips and started singing. He didn't stick around after that.

Principal Kim came marching in with big first-day-of-school energy, waving at students like he was Santa Claus himself. His toothy grin blinded the audience. Theodore Kim was now a man in charge of the future. He felt powerful in a way he couldn't describe. But then, as he held a small stack of important-looking papers, his hands began to shake. His nerves kicked in, but he pushed through them. He had to. His students were counting on him. "Hello, everyone! I'd like to welcome you all . . ." His trembling voice stopped cold. The words he spent all night preparing simply didn't want to come out. An unruly student took advantage of the weak moment.

"Seventh grade sucks! Eighth grade rules!" a boy shouted. A few kids booed. Others clapped.

Boob nudged Rube. "Sixth graders don't even register as human beings. This is bad."

Principal Kim gulped in fear as paper airplanes, spitballs, and other unidentifiable items zoomed through the room. The assembly had turned into a war zone before it had even begun. He put on his imaginary general's cap and whipped things into shape. "THAT'S ENOUGH!" At last, Principal Kim had the room's undivided attention. Even the deaf students heard him. Impressed by his newfound bravery, he kept the ball rolling.

"Thank you. And welcome to the first day of school. I'm Principal Kim. Some of you may remember me from elementary school or, perhaps, one of the many other roles I've played in the community. Please don't ask me why Taco Cavern removed the chimichangas from their menu. You'll have to talk to the new manager, Misty, about that. Good luck. She's *not* very nice." He released a long, thoughtful sigh. "But enough about that! I'm very excited to usher you all into a brand-new year here at Beechwood Middle School, where dreams come true!" Now that that tension had melted from his body, Principal Kim finally felt in control. He just needed a little boost of encouragement. "Please clap." The students did what they were told, filling the gym with uproarious clapping. "We have

45

a fun new Juice Box Truck that'll be parked outside after school. I hope everyone has a chance to grab a zesty and flavorful treat. Low sugar content to boot! There are some delicious, mouthwatering flavors including"—Principal Kim looked down at his paper, his face twisting in disgust—"Blueberry Rambutan, Candy Cane, and . . . Tomato Prune?" He looked over at Miss Mary, who apologetically shrugged.

"Those flavor combinations are *foul*," Boob whispered in Rube's ear. "Rambutan *is* a real fruit, though. Looks like an alien egg. We should get some from the International Market downtown and make a pie or something."

In the middle of the gym, amid a vast sea of students, a single hand shot into the air trying to get Principal Kim's attention. It didn't wave frantically or bend itself into shapes, hoping to be seen. It simply stayed put. Like a beacon. And for the next five minutes, as Principal Kim droned on about rules and policies, the hand stayed raised. After a while, he couldn't help but address it. "To whoever has their hand up, this is not . . ." The hand lowered, and in its place stood a bright young woman. "Oh. Hello, Pearl."

When Pearl Williams had a question, she asked it. Didn't matter if she was in a class of twenty people or one hundred. Fear wasn't a word in her vocabulary. It's not that she particularly liked challenging authority. Pearl was more about clarity. She needed to know the hows and the whys when it came to matters of the community. If adults were making decisions about her future, she needed answers.

"Aha," Rube muttered. *There she is.* He'd been looking for her all morning.

"Congrats on the glow up, Principal Kim," she said, beaming. "You made it to the big leagues."

Principal Kim blushed. A little bit of flattery went a long way. "I did, didn't I? Thank you, Pearl. That's very kind to say."

"Who's going to fix our school?" she asked bluntly. "It's kind of falling apart."

The unexpected and direct question hit Principal Kim right in the gut. "Um, well, uh . . ." he stammered. He looked over to Miss Mary for help, but she pretended to take a phone call.

"I noticed the wheelchair ramps were blocked this morning," Pearl noted. "Respectfully, sir, our differently abled students need more access. What will be done about that?"

Principal Kim smiled as best he could, but mostly his face looked like he'd just bitten into a frozen pizza. "Pearl. It's the first day of school."

"And we're excited! I think it'll be a *great* year," Pearl proclaimed. "But I also had a question about our clubs and teams. In the past, students have been forced to sell bootleg candy, plastic

flower arrangements, and faulty electric candles if they wanted to join an organization. Will that be happening again, or does our district have the resources to fund our extracurricular activities, so families don't need to pay out of pocket? And what about the STEM program we were promised?"

"No one cares!" shouted a boy in the back of the room. "Sit down, loudmouth!"

"My mouth is loud because yours stays shut." *Nothing fazes her.* "Principal Kim, do you have a plan to deal with *bullies*? Or should I handle this one myself?"

"Whoever made that rude comment needs to understand that we *respect* each other here at Beechwood Middle. Now let's continue on with the assembly," he replied, growing impatient. "It's not the time to bring up these kinds of issues, Pearl."

"When is a good time?" Pearl pulled a small day planner out of her pocket. "I have some availability tomorrow."

"Ahem!" Principal Kim cleared his throat as he searched for the right words. "Pearl, I truly appreciate your *vigor* with regard to these matters. New initiatives like the Juice Box Truck will help fund all the things that need funding. We're doing everything we can with the resources we have. That's all I can say at the moment."

"The flavors sound gross!" someone shouted.

"We're counting on you, sir." Pearl said. "*All of us.*"

Principal Kim was touched by the heartfelt sentiment. "Pearl, you and I will have a discussion just as soon as humanly possible."

"I look forward to it," Pearl said. She sat back down, pleased by the bit of progress.

"Moving on! Some of our traditional events and gatherings will be slightly different this year. We're still having the Harvest Festival, Switcheroo Dance, and our famous Beechwood Bandicoot Day. But the Science Fair has officially been canceled . . ."

Rube's heart sank deep into his chest as if being swallowed by a black hole. He felt like throwing up. The Science Fair was the only thing he'd remotely looked forward to in the new year. Weirdly, he didn't understand just *how much* he'd looked forward to it until this very moment. "You can't do this to me!!!" he blurted out. All the students turned and looked at him. It would've been embarrassing if not for the fact that he didn't care what they thought.

Boob tapped him on the shoulder. "You're thinking out loud again," he whispered.

"Let me finish my statement," said Principal Kim. "Even though the Science Fair has been canceled, that doesn't mean we're not starting the school year off with a bang."

CRASH!!!

Out of nowhere, one of the gym's large hanging lights fell to the ground behind Principal Kim, shattering unexpectedly. The

light's metal caging kept most of the sharp bulb fragments from escaping across the floor, but the sight was still jarring. While no one was actually hurt, the sudden event left Principal Kim shaken.

"Gladys the Ghost is going to kill us!" Boob yelled. No one knew what he was talking about, but that didn't stop the room from completely freaking out. Some kids thought it was a prank, while others grew frightened. As teachers and aides scurried to clean up the mess, Mike and Ike grabbed their phones and began recording. The room quickly devolved into craziness, which made Rube hyperventilate. The anarchy was too much to for him to handle.

"The school *is* falling apart!"

"Pearl was right! Pearl for president!"

"Those juice box flavors *are* gross!"

Principal Kim desperately tried to regain control, raising his voice to quiet the ruckus. "*As I was about to say*, the Science Fair has been canceled to make way for something *big*, something *bold*, and something *new*. I'm proud to announce Beechwood Middle School's First Annual Contraption Convention! Also known as Con-Con, trademark pending."

What's this? Rube's eyes widened with curiosity.

"Students are being challenged to create and build an original invention or unique contraption that performs a simple task. To compete, all you need is a great imagination!"

My time has come. Rube's heart started beating out of his chest. This was way better than a Science Fair. *Waaaay better.* It was a chance for Rube to show off his new skills as a builder. His brain burst with ideas.

"This is *not* just a solo endeavor. We want to see teamwork, tenacity, improvisation, and real problem-solving. I want all of you to think about what that truly means. Sign-up begins tomorrow morning. Our new science teacher, Mr. Blank, will be overseeing the competition. I hope all of you will think outside the box, reach for new heights, and . . ." He grabbed a T-shirt from a nearby box and held it up without looking first to see what it said. Giggles from the audience informed him of an oversight. "*Be Bland?* These were supposed to say *Be Bold*!" He looked for Miss Mary, but she was nowhere to be found. "Once these are fixed, everyone will be getting one. Oh, and the grand prize! I almost forgot. The winner of Con-Con will have their photo in the *Beechwood Chronicle*, a shout-out on social media from Greggles the Gadget Guy, a trophy, of course, and a gift card from Taco Cavern!"

· Boob was unimpressed. "*Lame*," he said, nudging Rube. "We should make a spaceship. Or a go-kart. Or both! I'm game to build a Transformer if you are."

Rube stayed suspiciously silent. He didn't want to hurt Boob's feelings. But he also wasn't keen on working in a group. *Nope. Not doing that.*

Principal Kim noticed Mike and Ike recording the presentation with their phones. "Put those away. Beechwood Middle School has a very strict NO PHONES policy. Violators will face punishment. If you see something, say something. And if you say something, *speak clearly.* I'm not an interpreter. And that concludes our assembly. Let's make this the best year ever, okay? Go, Bandicoots!" Principal Kim raced out of the gym as fast as he could to avoid any additional drama. Students went to lunch, buzzing about what they'd just seen and heard. Some were excited, others intrigued. An annoyed group of eighth-grade boys talked about organizing a video game competition instead. But none of them had the energy to actually do it.

Boob made a beeline for the cafeteria. "Gotta grab a pizza bagel before they sell out. I'll save you a seat."

Before he could eat, Rube had business to attend to. Pearl was at the other end of a very crowded hallway. Realizing he'd never catch her in time, Rube resorted to desperate measures.

"HEY!" His full-throated bellow made everyone turn around at once. The power of puberty was in full effect. Even *he* was surprised by the magnitude. "Oh. Um, that was for her." He pointed over the crowd to where Pearl was standing. It had been months since he'd seen her. She was taller than he remembered but her smile was as bright as ever. Though something about her style and demeanor had changed. They'd been friends for a long time, but now, all of a sudden, Rube looked at her with new eyes. As he made his way through the parted crowd, a weird sound bubbled up from his stomach. *Be quiet, you. Now is not the time.* He greeted Pearl with a humble grin.

"Well, well, well," Pearl said. "The infamous RGLG."

"I've been looking for you all day. Didn't see you at the bike racks this morning."

"I got here super early to volunteer in the school garden."

"Our school has a garden?"

"Yep. But no one's been taking care of it, so me and a couple other people are refurbishing the whole thing. Planting new stuff. You want to help?"

"Um, not really."

"Mmmmm-hmmmm."

"You look really nice. I mean, not that you don't usually, but, um, that outfit is very crisp and, um, professional." *Maybe I shouldn't talk for a minute.*

"Thanks. I stayed up all night picking through hundreds of outfits just so I could receive a compliment from a boy."

"Really?" *Winner winner chicken dinner!*

"Absolutely not." *Never mind.* She let the awkward moment linger between them, knowing that sort of stuff drove Rube mental.

"That Con-Con thing sounds cool."

"Yeah. I thought so too. I hope I can make it work with Chess Team. And Book Society. And volunteering at the soup kitchen downtown. But is that really what you want to talk about while there's an elephant in the room?"

Rube looked over each of his shoulders. "I thought I smelled something funny."

"Always with the jokes." Pearl shook her head. "You're a *real* one, Goldberg."

"Did you pack lunch, or are you buying?" Rube asked. A quick change of subject always did the trick. "I heard they make a killer pizza bagel at this place. And the chocolate milk is supposedly to die for. *Literally*. It's poison."

"My dad made me a PB&J."

"Fancy. Boob and I are going to sit in the corner by the poster that says LET'S TALK and has a picture of a zebra and a caterpillar on it. We'll save you a seat."

"Thanks, but that's okay. I'm actually having lunch in the library."

"Oh." Rube knew something was off with Pearl, but he absolutely, without a doubt, did *not* want to have to talk about it. *Better to ignore the situation and hope it goes away.* It wasn't that he didn't care about Pearl's well-being. He did. *Very much.* But talking about uncomfortable stuff made him feel uncomfortable, and he *hated* that more than anything.

Once his feelings were out in the open, he was vulnerable. There was nowhere to hide, and he wasn't good at lying. At least, that's what he told himself. His preferred method of deflection was to simply put on a happy face and pretend everything was fine until someone backed him into a corner and forced him to have a difficult conversation. But now, standing in front of Pearl, he realized he couldn't possibly spend the rest of the day wondering if he'd done something to hurt her. "Are you mad at me?"

Pearl sighed. Dealing with Rube's insecurities was her least favorite thing to do. There was a time and a place for everything, and, in a few hours, their issues would all be sorted. At least, that was the plan. "We'll talk about it at the Lair."

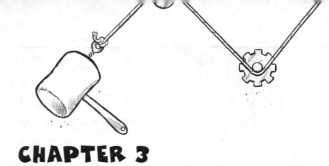

CHAPTER 3

The rest of the day was torture. There were way too many things on Rube's mind for him to actually concentrate. When the final bell rang, he raced out the door to meet his friends like a bat out of hell. Con-Con had unleashed a surge of thoughts. He wanted to go home right away and start building something. *Anything.* There were a million ideas in his notebook and no time to waste. He fished it out of his backpack and flipped through it as he walked. Most of his machines were loose, untested concepts. He had to choose a few solid options and perform trials to make sure they worked properly. From there, he'd select one to build for the convention. After that? A big win and international acclaim! Distracted by plan-hatching, his face buried in his notebook, Rube stopped paying attention to where he was going and walked right into a tree.

"Hahahaha!" Lala cackled. She was sitting in her limo with the window rolled down, watching Rube from afar. "C'mere, Goldberg. I wanted to talk to you."

Suddenly, Bertha bounded into the schoolyard, jumping onto Rube like a beast. She licked his hands and nuzzled his legs with absolute joy. Lala, however, was repulsed. "Where'd that thing come from?"

"She's not a thing. This is Bertha," Rube said, crouching down to show his pooch some love. "I built a machine that's timed to open her doggy door so she can use the bathroom. She must have gotten anxious and followed my scent all the way here. Guess I shouldn't have filled my pockets with bacon bits. Haha."

"That's disgusting." Lala winced.

Before Rube could explain that he was joking about the bacon bits, Bertha leaped up and began licking Lala's face without stopping. Rolex wasn't having any of that. The agitated cat launched out of the limo like a cannonball, attaching himself to Bertha's back. *RAOWR! ARF? RAOWR!* The two animals rolled across the courtyard, tussling. To the naked eye, they looked playful, but Rolex was out for blood. When a kid jokingly threw a dollar bill onto the ground, Lala's chauffeur, Hives, dressed in his driving uniform, exited the vehicle and took control of the situation.

"Rolex Chanel Givenchy Palooza the Second, return to this vehicle at once! If you fail to comply, I shall be forced to destroy your feline condominium and deny you any and *all* catnip privileges for a fortnight. Disobey me at your own leisure." Rolex knew when he was beaten. He'd never dream of risking that sweet, sweet catnip. With the battle concluded, he said goodbye to Bertha with a chipper meow and hopped back into safety of the limo. "Unleashed dogs are against the law, Mr. Goldberg. Do something about *yours*."

"On it." Rube gave Hives an awkward salute. "Hey, Lala, want to come to the Lair with me, Boob, and Pearl?"

Lala cringed. "Are you insane? The last time you dragged me into the woods, I smelled like twigs and leaves for a week. No, thanks." She put her hair behind her ears and cleared her throat. "Look, I need to talk to you. Soon. I want to collab sometime."

Rube didn't know what she was talking about, but he went

with it. "Yeah, sure, I'd love to collab. I do them a lot . . . collabing . . . and stuff . . ."

"*Perf*. I'll be in touch. Au revoir!" Lala rolled her window up as the limo drove away. The students of Beechwood Middle were left mesmerized as usual. Pearl and Boob had been watching from nearby. Now that the show was over, they joined Rube at the bike rack.

"What was that all about?" Pearl asked.

"Lala wants to collab!" Rube exclaimed. "Whatever that means."

"Collab is short for *collaboration*," Pearl replied. "She wants to work with you on something. But why?"

"She knows genius when she sees one."

"Excuse me . . ." The boy with the black hair from earlier that morning needed to get his bike from the rack. "Would you mind?"

Boob was standing in the way.

"Oops! Sorry," Boob said, moving to the side.

The boy struggled to dislodge his old ten-speed, but the rusty thing was stuck. He gave it a quick, forceful yank that sent Bertha into a tizzy. She barked and growled at the boy, thinking her master and his friends were in danger.

"Cut it out!" Rube scolded. Something about the boy was curious and awkward. He didn't seem to know his way around. Major *new kid* vibes. For a brief moment, Rube thought about inviting him along. *A nice gesture.* But today wasn't the day for those. *Maybe another time.* Aggravated by Bertha's outburst, the boy took off down the street and went about his business.

"Where are your bikes?" asked Pearl.

"Long story," Boob replied.

"Then I guess we're tripling up," Pearl said, hopping onto her ride. Rube carefully positioned himself on the front of her bike while Boob clumsily positioned himself on the back. "Hold on. And

do *not* try any funny business." As Pearl pedaled, the weight of the two boys caused her to swerve across the sidewalk. Bertha, ever the faithful sidekick, gleefully galloped beside them as they headed to their destination. Getting there wasn't the easiest. It was down a winding hill, across a bridge, past Stoffregen Farm, near the old factory district, over by the river. But

that only got you to the entrance to the forest. From there, you had to follow a semisecret trail leading to a small clearing where their secret sanctuary sat peacefully among the trees.

Three summers ago, Rube and Boob wanted a clubhouse. They wanted a place to meet, hang out, play games, etcetera. The plan was to convince one, or both, of their families that their backyards were the perfect location for such a thing. But no amount of begging and pleading made that happen. Bothered but undeterred, the boys hatched a new plan. They'd build their clubhouse in a secret place, where no one could find it. After scouting locations all over town, they finally settled on a quiet little spot in the middle of the Beechwood Forest. The place was thick with leafy overgrowth that made the area dark and mysterious. Rube and Boob began spiriting away pieces of salvageable wood from local abandoned buildings. It took them a few weeks to collect what they needed. Then Rube drew up some crude schematics, and they started building. Pearl stepped in to help when a few problems cropped up. Her dad was an architect, so she knew what she was doing. After working in secret for months, their clubhouse masterpiece was finally finished. A quaint little shack in the woods, though a debate raged over what to call it. Rube liked the Party Hut, while Pearl was partial to the Hidden Thicket. Boob demanded that they call it the Lair. No one had the energy to challenge him.

In the beginning, Rube, Boob, and Pearl spent a lot of time at the Lair. It was a safe house. A place to get away from nagging parents and annoying siblings. But they weren't playful little explorers any longer. Young adulthood was on the horizon. But there was one tradition they held on to—the first-day-of-school gabfest. That's when they talked about new classes, teachers, and anything else that was on their mind. It was a way to compare notes and figure out which classmates to avoid in the coming year.

"Whoa."

They arrived at the Lair to find it desperately in need of fixing. Summer storms had ravaged the place, covering it in branches and

leaves. The wood had rotted, making the air inside it damp and mossy. Otherwise, it was the same old place they knew and loved. Boob ran to the corner of the room where a blue tarp covered a large item. He yanked it off and made a grand discovery.

"My bike!" he exclaimed. "I forgot I left it here the other night when I was hanging by myself."

Rube felt the floor to make sure it was sturdy. "The floorboards are a little warped from the water damage. Be careful as you step. Guess it's been a while since I've been here."

"You think?" Pearl said, exchanging side-eyed looks with Boob.

"This place is a mess, Boob," Rube said. "Why didn't you tell me? I could have come here and done repairs over the summer."

"You've been doing your own thing. I didn't want to bother you." Boob took a seat and stretched his arms out on the table, flexing his fingers in giddy anticipation. "Shall we begin?" Going over school gossip was one of Boob's favorite things in the world. It was a way for him to release all the stored knowledge he'd accumulated throughout the day. He was cursed to notice everything

and everyone. Little details lodged themselves in his brain. Now he could finally release them into the wild.

"Jimmy Frankenplatz cracked his tooth on a diving board but hasn't gotten it fixed yet, so he has one weird, sharp, Dracula tooth. Don't ask him about it. He'll get mad."

"They gave us this booklet in health class called *Changes Are Coming.* I'm not reading it. I don't care if I fail! Too scary."

"Zizi Baz puked in German class. It was *brutto.*"

"There are no doors on the bathroom stalls by the library. *None.* It's the worst."

"Did you know we have, like, a million clubs? The Guidance Office has flyers about them. I think might join the Book Society, but only if there's not a lot of reading. There's also a club called the Gay-Straight Alliance, which sounds like it's got a cool *Star Wars* thing going on. I'll definitely be checking that one out once I finish making my Chewbacca costume."

"The spring musical is the *Loin King.* Wait. Maybe I read that wrong."

"Candace Winterbottom said her parents are paying for her to launch a fragrance line. She's dating Ryan now too. They share their social media accounts. Like *that'll* end well."

"Oh! And Ronnie Lopez goes by Reina now, so make sure you use the right pronouns."

"Good for her," said Pearl. "That makes me happy."

"Yeah, that's cool." Rube was ready to move on. "Are we done yet?"

"Just one more thing," Boob said, rubbing his palms together feverishly. "What are we making for Con-Con? Obviously the three of us are a team, right?"

"Of course," Pearl said. "Let's figure out a plan of attack."

Rube had been dreading this moment since the minute Con-Con had been announced. Machine building was *his* gig. He didn't want to do it with anyone else, and yes, that included his friends. *They don't understand how things work! They'll just get in the way. Gotta let them down softy. They'll understand. It'll be fine. Right?* Seconds passed as Rube considered his options. Making a big splash at Con-Con on his own was his top priority. Explaining to his friends that he wasn't interested in being part of a team wasn't going to go over well, but it *had* to happen. *That's just how it has to be.* What else could he do except rip the Band-Aid off and get it over with? "I'm entering by myself. No offense or anything."

"That doesn't make sense," Pearl said. "The whole point of the competition is to work together. You heard Principal Kim, right?"

"Yeah but, it's just that, I want to do it on my own." Rube had really stepped in it now. There was nothing left to do but keep going. "You two can be a group without me just fine. It's not mandatory anyway."

"We want to do this with you," Boob said. "What's your problem?"

Rube was getting agitated. "*I* don't have a problem. Pearl's the one who has a problem. Good luck getting her to commit, what with all the things *Lady Extracurricular* has going on."

This was the part where Boob tapped out. Tension between friends made him anxious and uncomfortable. He leaned down,

cupping his ear in Bertha's direction. "What was that, girl? You need a breath of fresh woodland air? Why yes, I'd love to take you on a walk." Bertha flashed her doofy grin and wagged her tail like a maniac. "Be back in a bit." They disappeared into the surrounding woods, leaving Rube and Pearl staring blankly at each other. It was time to talk. But Rube was too chicken to make the first move.

"You probably want to know how my summer was, right? Cool! I'll tell you. *It was one of the best of my life.* Thanks for asking." Pearl glowed as she remembered it. "It began with a family vacation to Mexico, where I got to swim with dolphins, snorkel in a reef that was overflowing with sea life—the colors were *amazing*— and enjoy the local culture. Back at home, I volunteered at the food bank downtown, went to my brother's baseball games, helped my mom repot all of her plants, and painted my room: royal blue. Did some cooking out with neighbors, had a few movie nights in the backyard, and even organized a bake sale. Oh yeah, I learned how to make banana bread! It's a lot simpler than you think. Used the money I made from the bread stand to buy myself a microscope, so, naturally, I started collecting insects. Thinking of starting a local astronomy club too. Only read ten and a half books, though. I wanted to read twelve, but time just got away from me. Other than that, it was fairly low-key. How was yours?"

She got me. Rube had walked into a trap of his own making.

On the last day of the previous school year, he and Pearl had made all kinds of summer plans. *Together.* Rube was supposed to volunteer, bake banana bread, and attend all those family cookouts. Pearl made him promise not to bail on her. But for reasons he couldn't articulately clearly, he completely dropped the ball. Pearl called and texted, yet Rube never picked up. One day, she even went by his house to say hello, but he hid in the basement and pretended no one was home. *Who does that!? Me, I guess.* He knew he'd behaved rudely. He knew he'd made a mistake. But that was only part of the story. Part of him just wanted to apologize and get it over with. The other part didn't feel like talking.

"It was fine" was all Rube could muster.

"Wow." Pearl deflated. She wasn't there to play games. "That's *all* you've got?"

"I don't know what else to say." *Yes, you do!*

"Say the truth! Why is that so difficult?"

"Okay, fine. I hung out in my room and built stuff. Happy now?"

"What kind of stuff?"

"Machines. Stuff that can help people, I guess. Or whatever."

"Like an irrigation system that could revolutionize farming?"

"Uhhh. Not exactly."

"So, what then?"

"A machine that helps you fold your underwear."

"Uh-huh. So *that's* why you ghosted me all summer?"

"I know that sounds weird. And bad."

"I mean . . ." Pearl shrugged. "You didn't ghost *Boob*."

"Yeah, but he's different, and it's not like we went anywhere. Boob just came over to my house." With every utterance, Rube dug himself further into a hole that was slowly becoming a shallow grave. *Change the subject, change the subject, change the subject.* He scanned his brain for relevant topics. The weather? *Dumb.* The finale of *Talentstorm U.S.A.?* Didn't watch. Also, *dumb.* What about a nice, well-placed compliment? *Ah, now that's an excellent idea! Just don't mention her outfit again.* "It was really cool when you stood up in front of the whole school and owned Principal Kim."

Pearl shook her head and rolled her eyes at the same time. "I wasn't trying to own anyone. All I wanted were answers. Everyone knows our school needs help, but not enough people are doing something about it. Sometimes adults say one thing and do another. It drives me crazy. One of the things I learned in the past few months is that if anything is going to get done around here, *we* have to be the ones to do it."

"I mean, sure, there are things that need doing, but not *that* much doing."

Pearl was tired of playing Rube's games. "Are we done yet?

There are a million other places *Lady Extracurricular* could be right now."

Ouch. Rube wasn't sure what to say next. *Tell her about the weird dream you had where you were both living in an old steam engine. It didn't make sense, but it might make her laugh?*

As Rube's distracted mind wandered, a flood of memories came rushing into his thoughts. Images and reminders of his friendship with Pearl from over the years. Like doing karaoke performances for their stuffed animals back when they were little. Or that time they found a turtle on the side of the road after it got hit by a car. Pearl named her Tortuga, nursed her back to health, and set her free in the woods a week later. *I wonder if she's around here somewhere, watching us.* Last year, Pearl planned Rube a surprise birthday party, but no one came because she got the dates mixed up. They ended up eating a carrot cake all by themselves. But that didn't really matter. Pearl made the thing, so it was delicious. *Say something, Goldberg. You're acting like a quiet zombie right now.*

"For what it's worth, I'm sorry I ruined your summer."

"Were you not listening to me, Goldberg? My summer was awesome. It's just a shame that it didn't include one of my best friends. That's all."

GRRRRRR! BARK! BARK, BARK! GRRRRRR!

"Get over here!" Boob screamed. "Bertha found a dead body!"

Rube and Pearl scrambled out of the Lair and into the woods, where Bertha had discovered something curious behind a giant fallen tree. Boob kept his distance, peeking at the scene through his mask of fingers. No one wanted to get too close. The only thing that was visible was a piece of soiled white fabric that clearly belonged to a dress. Bertha angrily bit down, dragging an old doll out from behind the piece of timber. Its body was soft, damp, and covered in small toadstools. Its hair was patchy. Stuffing poured from its stomach. The doll's face had been mangled, though its eyes remained penetrating. The thing had been rotting in the forest for a very long time. Bertha dropped the doll and sat beside it,

proud of her bizarre discovery.

"Yuck," Pearl said, holding her nose. "That thing stinks."

Boob started shaking. The sight of the doll sent shivers through his body. "That grimy old doll is dressed just like Gladys the ghost girl." He ran over to his backpack and retrieved the book he'd checked out earlier in the day. "There's a picture in here somewhere." He furiously flipped through the pages, looking for the photograph in question.

"There's no such thing as . . ." Pearl stopped short of saying the G-word. She didn't want to upset Boob any more than he already was. "It's probably just a coincidence."

"*I'm telling you*: Something weird is going on."

A gust of wind swept through the trees, making them rustle and sway. Rube's mind started wandering. Not about ghosts or supernatural occurrences. He looked out across the forest and saw nature's machines, working in harmony. There were pulleys, planes, and levers. As he stared at the ecosystem, his head swelled with new ideas. He knew his friends would be mad if he up and left, but in his mind, he had no choice but to ride the wave of inspiration.

"I'm really sorry about this," Rube said, hopping onto Boob's bike. "C'mon, girl!" He took off down the trail, with Bertha following closely behind. His final words reverberated through the forest. "I'll make it up to you very soon!"

Boob was completely crestfallen. "Did he just take my bike?"

"That he did, my friend." Pearl put her hand on his shoulder. "What are we going to do with Rube Goldberg?"

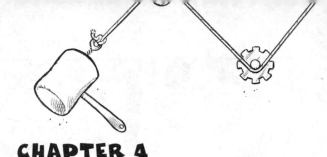

CHAPTER 4

"C'mon, c'mon, c'mon . . ."

Rube was on the verge of a nervous breakthrough. He'd been sketching machines and tinkering with ideas for hours. On an empty stomach, no less. That made the voices in his head a tad more confusing than usual. He had to figure out what to build for Con Con, but he just couldn't make up his mind. *It has to be spectacular!* But also practical. *It's got to offer a solution to a preexisting problem!* And look good while doing it. *This machine has to be EVERYTHING.* But "everything" was a tough expectation to meet and a recipe for implosion. Instead of unraveling his brain jumble, he scrapped all of his previous work and started fresh. It was better that way. New stuff always got him excited anyway. He began digging through boxes, looking for parts, despite not knowing what exactly he was making. Then came the pile making. Levers over here. Wedges over there. Wheels on the bed. Planes on the desk. And mounds of miscellaneous stuff to bring it all together. He

opted not to sketch this one. Instead, he searched for cool parts and began assembling an unknown machine. As he built, its function revealed itself in the making. *A juicer.* He named his newest creation the Juicy Lucy.

"Stay back, Bertha," Rube demanded. "Don't screw this up for me *again*."

Offended by Rube's suggestion, Bertha sat patiently in the corner, even though she was desperate to bound around the room like a lunatic.

"Here we go!"

Rube set the Juicy Lucy in motion, hovering over it closely. He needed to see how every single part worked in unison. It helped him understand how to fix problem areas. Suddenly, halfway through the trial run, the machine faltered. Rube had unknowingly miscalculated one of the steps. His newest work instantly fell into ruin.

"No. NO. NO!"

Frustrated by the failure, Rube wrecked the machine in an angry outburst, kicking its parts and sending them flying across his room in all directions. Emotional eruptions never helped him be a better builder, but sometimes he just couldn't help them. Bertha watched the whole thing unfold from her perch in the corner. After Rube collected himself, he sat down on the ground and called her over for a little snuggle. But Bertha wouldn't budge.

"Maybe teamwork isn't such a bad idea after all."

In the corner of the bedroom, Rube's laptop began playing a song. A video call was coming through. He wasn't sure he wanted to answer it but did anyway. "Hey, Dad. What's up?"

"Hey, buddy! How was your first day of middle school?"

Max Goldberg did the best he could with what he had. Putting food on his family's table was always his top priority. More often than not, that meant going on long business trips. As a traveling salesman, his job was to convince people they needed stuff. He was good at it too. People adored his bubbly spirit. Max never took advantage of his customers, and for that, they rewarded him. But

he missed Rube desperately, and there was little he could do to remedy the situation.

"It was okay. Lots of changes. Blah, blah, blah."

With his father gone so much, Rube was by himself a lot—though he wasn't technically unsupervised. Max had installed security cameras throughout the house to monitor Rube's comings and goings. He didn't like invading his son's privacy like that, but it had to be done for his protection. What Max didn't know was that Rube rewired the whole system while he was gone. When Max checked the cameras, something he did once a day, what he *really* saw was old footage on a loop that played over and over again. He never knew the difference.

"Grandma said she left you a cheesy potato casserole in the fridge," Max said. "Have you eaten yet? You need to eat, Rueben. I don't want you up all night building stuff on an empty stomach."

Rube's Grandma Etta lived in a small cottage in the backyard. She was a sweet lady who kept to herself. Her health was stellar. When she wasn't playing mah-jongg at the weekly meeting of the Tuesday Ladies Club, she was napping. Grandma Etta mostly popped into the house when Rube wasn't around. She loved him very much, but they kept very different schedules.

"I will, I will, I will," Rube groaned. For a twelve-year-old boy, he was surprisingly self-sufficient. But that didn't mean he took care of himself.

"Talk to me," Max said. "What's all that mess happening in your room?"

"I'm just fooling around. Nothing big."

Rube almost mentioned Con-Con. *Almost.* But he knew his dad would be upset that he wasn't there to help Rube. So he'd wait and tell his dad about it once that first-place trophy was sitting on their kitchen table. *Hopefully.*

"You seem down, buddy."

"I'm not down, just frustrated about something."

"Ah. Teachers already piling on the homework, eh?"

"Something like that."

"Why don't you take Bertha for a walk? Clear your head a little bit."

"Good idea. Maybe we'll go over to the Haunted Hideaway and

see what's shakin'."

Max wasn't amused. "Stay away from that place, Rube. I'm being serious. I know you're fascinated, but that yard is a legitimate hazard. You'll hurt yourself. Do you understand?"

"When are you coming home?"

The question always broke Max's heart. "I'm going to be away for a little longer than I thought. Lots of new opportunities coming my way. We'll be set for life if everything goes according to plan." Rube stared deadpan at his father. "Rube? Did the computer freeze?"

"The computer is fine," said Rube. *But I'm not.*

"I'll make it up to you when I'm back home, okay? I promise. We'll go over to Mr. Riesman's junkyard and grab a whole bunch of cool stuff to tinker with. Just like you, me, and Mommy did back when you were little. Remember that?" A buzzing phone stole Max's attention. "Look, I've got to go. Work is calling. If you need anything and Grandma is sleeping, just got to Bonnie and Phil's next door. They said you and Bertha can stay in their guest room if you want. That might be fun! Love you, buddy. Talk soon."

And with that, Max was gone. Rube looked over at Bertha perched under the windowsill. She was sound asleep for the most part, except for her legs, which twitched as she dreamed As he bent down to pet her, he noticed the Haunted Hideaway in the distance. *What if I jimmied open the gate and swiped that handsome accordion rack?* Stealing wasn't usually something Rube did, but this was different. *I'm liberating a piece of art!* Rube dug through his desk drawer and found an old piece of mail. *A little insurance. Just in case.* He stuffed it in his back pocket, kissed Bertha on the snout, and hightailed it out the door. *This is so exciting.* It wasn't disobeying orders that gave him a rush, it was that he might actually get answers to questions that had nagged him since he was five years old. It was well worth the twinge of guilt he felt for breaking his dad's rule.

As Rube approached the property, he analyzed the fence that surrounded it. *Not as flimsy as it looks from far away. I could probably climb this if I had to.* The front gate was already, weirdly, ajar. *What luck! Or a trap.* He trekked up the hill, trudging through the wasteland of junk and scrap. To him it was a dream. A salvage yard full of machine parts. There was an old mechanical fan, a lasso, a mallet, a box of stuffed animals, an umbrella, toy trains, birdcages, a beekeeper suit, two watering cans, a dollhouse, a baseball mitt, a rusty coatrack, false teeth, lunchboxes, an ironing board, a tangled kite, four cannonballs, a broken flagpole, and a toilet plunger. But that stuff wasn't why he was there. He was there for that delicious collapsible accordion rack. It was totally old-school (his favorite kind of school) and perfect for one of the machines he'd been thinking

about. He tiptoed over to his prize and gave it a once-over. *Look at you, my beauty. A diamond in the rough. I'm going to take you home, clean you up, and give you purpose like never before. Come to Papa.* As he grabbed the accordion rack, a tiny green laser suddenly appeared on his hand. *What the—?!*

SCHAZAAAP!

"*Aieee!!!*" A shock traveled through Rube's body that left him trembling. *Maybe this wasn't such a good idea.* He followed the laser's origin point to a window in the third-floor attic of the Haunted Hideaway, where a figured loomed in the darkness. Rube, still smarting from the laser's sting, found himself feeling slightly braver than he was when he arrived.

"Hey!" he screamed. "Watch it!" *Inside voice, Rueben. Do you want to get yourself killed?* But then he thought about it for a moment. *You know what? No. Shooting lasers at kids doesn't work for me.* Rube stomped up the steps and gave the thin, paneled door a hearty whack. After a minute passed with no answer, he pressed the doorbell, which didn't work. Rube shuffled around the cluttered porch, peeking into the windows, but the dark curtains had been drawn. The place was seemingly impenetrable. *Wait a minute.* Rube noticed a brass knocker, shaped like a demon's head, on the front door. The thing was placed extraordinarily high, causing him to miss it the first time around. *I hate being a shorty.* He leaped up to grab it but couldn't make contact. *If at first you don't succeed, try, try again.* After a handful of passionate attempts, Rube finally got his hands on the knocker and swung it against the door with force.

TIK, TIK, TIK. CA-THUNK!

He'd inadvertently initiated a chain reaction that caused the door panels to move and switch places with one another, flipping and turning, over and over again. *It's . . . a . . . machine.* When the mechanism finished its transformation, a rusty steel door stood revealed. Nestled in the middle was a tiny little window, the size of a slice of cheese. Rube leaned in close and peered inside. "Hello?" he whispered.

"Who the @#$& are you?!" a voice roared from inside the house.

"*Gah!*" Rube tripped and fell backward onto his butt. A pair of crazy eyes stared at him through the tiny window. He was scared, sure, but also captivated. *Keep it together, Goldberg. The guy has lasers.* "Um, uh, my name is Rube. I live down the street."

"What are you selling? Flowers?! Greeting cards!? Cheese and sausage?! Whatever it is, I don't want any! Children begging people for money to help pay for their band or drama club or whatever stupid thing their school won't give them money for—it's a disgrace!"

"Couldn't agree more. But I'm not selling cheese and sausage. And I can't play an instrument to save my life. Though I do own a harmonica. It was a gift from—"

"You tried to steal from me!"

"Technically, yes. But I can explain! Got a minute to talk?"

"Ah. *I see.* You're here with literature about a *higher being.* You want me to bow down before your lord and master, eh? Peddle your mythology elsewhere, child. I reject it!"

"*Hoo boy,*" Rube murmured to himself. "That's *not* what this is about."

"If you need to talk to someone, find a therapist!"

Rube removed the envelope from his pocket and held it high. He was done playing games. "*I know who you are, Professor Butts.* Quit stalling and open the dang door."

The door slowly creaked open (on its own) as a balding man riding a motorized scooter zoomed toward Rube at super speed, stopping right at the edge of the doorway. He was an imposing gentleman with a bushy mustache and patchy, grey hair. The man eyed Rube suspiciously. "What's in your pockets?"

Rube turned his pockets inside out, and a single dried pepperoni fell out of one. "That's not mine. I don't know where that came from." A chipmunk leaped from behind a nearby bush, snatched the meat niblet, and scurried away happily.

"Children are disgusting little animals," the Professor grumbled. "Give me that envelope."

Rube waved it through in the air like he was conducting an orchestra. "Absolutely! But only if you let me inside. Those are the rules. Feel free to call the cops if you want. I'd be happy to tell them how you fired laser beams at me," he said, grinning from ear to ear.

"That's blackmail!" the Professor shouted.

Rube examined the envelope thoroughly. "Looks like *white* mail to me. But what do I know? I'm just a disgusting little animal."

The Professor's angry glare was speckled with curiosity. He didn't know what to make of Rube. Like any good scientist, he chose to study his subject so that he could conduct a full and through analysis. "You've got five minutes."

Rube entered the Haunted Hideaway carefully. No matter how confident he felt in his ability to run away at a moment's notice, this was still a stranger's house. The Professor led him down a long, dark hallway, floorboards creaking as they stepped. The deeper they went, the more the musty air smelled spicy. Birds squawked behind closed doors. The lights were covered in cobwebs. *Just like a real haunted house.* Rube wondered if he'd make a horrendous mistake.

"You're not going to trap me here like Dracula did to Jonathan Harker, right? I'm warning you in advance, my dog has an acute sense of smell. She'd find me in a second"—Rube rethought his words a bit—"when she's done growling at a bug or eating garbage."

"A fan of Bram Stoker's *Dracula*, eh? That's a bit advanced for a boy your age," the Professor mused. "But trust me when I tell you, I don't want your blood. I barely even want you in my home! This is simply my good deed for the day. No more, no less."

They turned a corner, entering a completely different wing of the home. It was an expansive living room workshop brimming with exotic items, wild inventions, and other bizarre paraphernalia. There were stacks of old newspapers piled high, leaning on one another so they wouldn't tip over. A spiral staircase twisted all the way up to a trapdoor in the ceiling. Strange machines were everywhere, with labels like the "Simplified Pencil Sharpener" and a "Machine for Washing Dishes While You Are at the Movies." *What is this place?*

While Rube was distracted, the Professor swiped the envelope from his grasp. "The date on this postmark is from five years ago."

"Is it? Oops. Guess I forgot to bring it over. My bad."

"It's a federal crime to steal another person's mail!"

"*Relax.* It's only junk mail. And it wasn't *stolen*. The mail carrier put it in my box by mistake." Rube floated through the room, noticing all its messy strangeness. Antique lamps sat on broken tables mended with packing tape. Clothes were piled in the corner like a fabric volcano. *Why are there empty cereal bowls everywhere?* Faint pops of grease crackled as chicken fried in the nearby kitchen. Rube was entranced by the disarray. The Professor's eyes followed him as he meandered around the room.

"So, *you're* Rueben Lucius Goldberg. Thought you'd be taller."

"Hold up," Rube said in a panicked tone. "How do you know who I am?"

"I know everything." The Professor flipped a piece of mail at Rube, hitting him in the face. "You're not the only federal criminal on the block."

"Touché! That's French for *I see what you did there.*"

"Let me guess," the Professor groaned. "You want to know where I got my funny name, is that it?"

"Nah. My best friend's named Boob. That stuff doesn't faze me. Hey, if you married his mom and adopted him, he'd be *Boob Butts*. That should *definitely* be illegal." Rube stared at the immense mess that surrounded him, shaking his head in disbelief. "You're a hoarder. Like on that TV show. *That's* why you've got all that stuff in your yard. Which is very cool, actually. The stuff, I mean, not the hoarding."

"I'm *not* a hoarder. All the items on my property are usable. I keep them around in case someone might have a *use* for them." He pointed at a box of tools in the corner. "Fetch me a dummy wrench, wouldja?"

"Sure thing." Rube bolted over to the box and began digging. "What does it look like?"

"You'll know when you see it."

Oh, you want to play games, huh? Rube poured the box out on the ground. Tools, machinery, and miscellaneous items scattered across the floor, much to the Professor's dismay.

"What the devil are you doing?!"

"There's no such thing as a *dummy* wrench. You just wanted to keep me busy while you figured out what I'm up to. Nice try, but I'm not some dumb, gullible kid." He rummaged through the pile of junk. "There's good stuff in here. You use this to make all your machines?"

The Professor didn't answer. Instead, he fired up his motorized scooter and zipped into the kitchen to continue preparing his dinner. As Rube put the odds and ends back into the box, he became distracted by the Professor's sweeping wall of accomplishments. *Man, this guy has lived a lot of life.* There were trophies, Certificates of Merit, and degrees from prestigious universities. Among shelves of paraphernalia sat framed photographs of family and friends in simpler times. One such group photo was marked with a seal and emblazoned with the words "International Science Council." Every item in the room had a story.

The Professor pointed to a teapot, sitting pretty on a pedestal in the corner. "While studying the rare and elusive four-toed sloth in the Yucatán rain forest, I stepped into quicksand and, while sinking, devised a simple idea for a three-legged teapot."

He added, "On a deep-sea dive in the South Pacific, doing research on the now-extinct striped jellyfish—close cousin to the spotted jellyfish—I devised a simple, automated mustache-trimming device. Never use the thing myself, but it works like a charm."

"This place is amazing," Rube said breathlessly. "*Messy*. But amazing."

"If you came here looking for a time-traveling car, I got rid of that in the 1980s."

"A fan of *Back to the Future*, eh? That's a bit simple for a man your age."

The Professor pantomimed a yawn. "Sick burn."

Amid his collection of nostalgia were newspaper clippings from the past that had become yellow like parchment. One headline read, in big bold letters, BUTTS TO ZEERO: "YOU'RE NO HERO!"

Under it was a photograph of the Professor in his younger days, facing off against a chubby gentleman with a bald head and a splotch-like birthmark on his cranium.

"Who's the cue ball?" Rube asked.

The question made the Professor testy. "You're currently surrounded by overwhelming evidence of my scientific brilliance. A lifetime's worth of accomplishment and adventure is before you, and yet you've chosen to ask *that*?" Rube shrugged. "He's Professor Tobias Zeero. A former colleague turned international criminal mastermind. We worked together on a top secret project that . . ." He paused for effect. "If I told you, I'd have to kill you. The man is a

fraud and a deceiver who threw me under a bus! Literally *and* figuratively. He's nothing but a stain on humanity. An agent of chaos."

"*Harsh.* Professor Zeero really did a number on you, huh?"

"It's not what he did to *me*, it's what he did to the people I love. *That* I'll never forgive. I had what he wanted, and he made my life hell because of it. Jealousy will eat a person alive, then spit their bones right back in their face."

"Yeesh." Rube winced. "What happened to him?"

"He's *dead*," the Professor said, offering up a plate of food. "Chicken wing? They're quite tangy." Rube wasn't interested. "Suit yourself." The Professor zipped over to his cluttered dinner table and began eating like an animal. "So, what are you doing with your life, Rueben? Playing video games? Eating french fries? Farting?"

"Video games are fine, but I'm into building machines. That's kind of why I came over here in the first place." *Just tell him the whole truth, dingus. This guy is on the level.* "I really wanted that accordion rack too. Oh, and I know who you *really* are, Professor, and all about your not-so-secret career. Have for a long time."

A chicken wing fell out of the Professor's mouth. "Is that so?"

"Don't worry, I haven't told anybody. We all call this place the Haunted Hideaway, since it looks abandoned. But I knew *someone* was living in here. After I accidentally got your mail, I did some digging online, but everywhere I looked just led me to dead ends. So I went all the way to the library downtown to look through old records. You're Lucifer Gorgonzola Butts. You used to be a famous inventor."

"I still am a famous inventor!" He pounded his fist onto the table.

"Sorry. I didn't mean anything bad. It's just that . . ." *How do I say this?* "You're not supposed to be alive. I think? Unless the records at the library are wrong. They didn't have nearly as many clippings and articles as you do."

"That's by design," the Professor snarled. "You look at me and see an old crackpot. Everyone in this town does. But I came here to change things for the better. *They're* the ones who wouldn't let me."

"They *who*?"

The Professor flung the plate of chicken wing bones into the nearby sink. "I'm just a phantom from the past, Rueben. You said it yourself. Don't pay me any mind."

Rube wasn't sure exactly how to proceed. An explosion of questions bounced around inside his head. *Is this guy in the middle of a breakdown? Am I going to end up in a dungeon? But for real, though, what are the chances he'll let me have that sweet accordion rack?* He decided to go with one of the more practical, albeit vague, options. "How do I build something that actually matters?"

"Come again?" The Professor frowned.

"You're a builder. You know what I'm talking about," said Rube. "It's really hard for me to concentrate sometimes. I can't stop thinking about machines and the way things work. I have so many ideas. There are so many problems to solve. But when I try to actually make something, it fails. Something always goes wrong. Nothing I make is good enough. All I want to do is build something that actually matters, so how . . . do . . . I . . . do that?"

The Professor guffawed so loudly he almost fell out of his chair. *"You're a child.* You're clever and capable, from what I can see, but give yourself a break, kid. Building something that matters takes time and consideration. First, you have to build something that *works.* Through trial and error. One step at a time. This is the builder's life. Get used to it."

Ask him. Do it. What have you got to lose? Do it now. Before he murders you.

"So, there's a machine-building competition at my school called Con-Con," Rube said, his voice shaking ever so slightly. "It would really be cool if you came."

"STOP!" the Professor shouted. "No. Not doing this. I'm not some aged automaton doling out advice to whatever mop-topped rug rat happens upon my doorstep."

"I don't know what that means." *You had to go and make him mad.*

The Professor cupped his hand to his mouth. "It means go ask your daddy for help," he whispered. "I'm not interested in being your mentor. People get paid for that sort of thing, and you want me to do it for free? Get lost, kiddo. You're out of your gourd."

"I didn't *ask* you to be my mentor, crankypants. I just needed someone to talk to, okay? As you're one of the world's most famous inventors, I thought maybe you could help me, but I guess when you stop doing the thing you love, it turns you into a jerk. Loosen up a little. It won't kill you."

The Professor remained silent, staring at Rube not with contempt but inquisitiveness. "I welcomed you into my home *despite* your attempted thievery. You are owed nothing by me or this world. Now it's time for you to go. My TV shows are almost on. Tonight is the finale of *American's Next Big Soft Drink*, and I've got money on cRaZy jUiCe taking the crown." He rose from his motorized scooter and stretched his arms as wide as they could go.

"You can walk?!"

He looked down at his legs and pretended to cry. "It's a miracle!" he exclaimed, dancing down the hallway like the pied piper. *This guy is so weird.* The Professor swung open the front door dramatically and stared at Rube. "Let's go! Chip-chop! I don't have all evening."

Rube took his sweet time strolling down the hallway, scrutinizing every inch of the Haunted Hideaway's eerie decor. "You know anything about ghosts in Beechwood?"

The Professor rubbed his chin. "Where do our spirits go when they leave our human shells? This is one of the great questions of existence. Energy cannot be created or destroyed. Only changed. You're into science, *you* figure out the rest. Or you could head over to the cemetery, put your ear to the ground, and see if you can hear any of the corpses trying to escape. Could be interesting, listening for the voices of the dead."

"I just might do that," Rube said. "The figuring out the science thing, I mean, not the listening for corpses." Strangely, he felt better than he did when he arrived at the Professor's home. Which was weird, considering the circumstances. Despite his cantankerous attitude, the Professor wasn't a bad guy. Misunderstood, maybe. Definitely mysterious. But not bad. Which is why Rube decided to make a last-ditch effort to retrieve the thing he came over there for in the first place. "So, can I have that accordion rack or what?"

"Not on your life," replied the Professor. He calmly removed a remote control from his pocket and pressed its only button. Suddenly, the hallway paneling slid away to reveal a series of mechanical arms that extended out like tentacles. One by one they latched onto Rube's limbs, lifting him into the air and gently tossing him out onto the porch. "Don't ever come here again," warned the Professor. "I'm being *serious*." The front door slammed shut as metal barriers lowered around each window. In an instant, the Haunted Hideaway had become an impenetrable fortress.

Rube didn't stick around to see what happened next. He ran back down the hill, through the garden of trash, all the way home. *What the heck just happened?!*

He didn't expect to find Boob sitting on the curb, waiting for him.

"What are you doing here?" Rube asked, his body still shaking.

"I was in the area," replied Boob. "Were you out walking Bertha?"

"Yep. Good ol' Bertha."

"Then where is she?" Boob asked.

Just tell him the truth. "Oh, she came home early."

Boob only half bought his excuse. "Hmm. Is my bike around here somewhere?"

"In the garage," Rube said. His breathing patterns were slowly returning to normal. The sight of his friend had calmed his nerves. "Wanna hang for a bit?"

"Sure."

They nabbed a bunch of

snacks from the kitchen, filling Rube's pant pockets with crispy, crunchy goodness. There was a spot on the roof that was perfect for stargazing. *Nice breeze.* No trees in the way of the sky. It faced the backyard too, so nosy neighbors wouldn't complain. The boys climbed out a second-story window and settled in.

"Did you figure out what you're making for Con-Con?"

"Not yet. But I've got a few ideas."

"Whatever it is, you'll win. I have a good feeling about it. You'll beat 'em all and reign supreme! Meanwhile, *I* may have unlocked dark, arcane forces by removing that creepy doll from the woods. According to the Internet, it's definitely possessed by the spirit of Gladys, the ghost girl. I'm bringing her to school tomorrow to see what else I can dig up."

"Spirit or not, that doll stuuuuuunk."

"Speaking of *ghosts*, you should really talk to Pearl. You ghosted her so hard, now she thinks *her* house is haunted." Boob waited for Rube's laugh, but it never materialized. "That's a good joke! It deserves at least a tiny giggle."

"Pearl is fine. And the joke was only so-so."

"You ghosted me too, to be honest."

"What are you talking about?! We hung out over the summer!"

"Yeah, but not that much. Not like we used to. Last summer, I basically lived at your house. If I ever got mail, I would've had it forwarded. Probably the best summer of my life. We dug a pond in your backyard! That eventually became a mud pit, because we didn't know what we were doing. Aw, man, was your dad mad about that. Sunbathing in the morning, afternoon naps on the couch watching cartoons. Endless cereal! Ahhhh, those were the days." Boob sighed as if he were an eighty-four-year-old man. "I guess growing up changes people."

Rube was getting visibly annoyed. "What do you want from me?" he asked, looking Boob directly in the face. It wasn't meant to make Boob uncomfortable, but it did.

Boob turned his head away and avoided Rube's gaze. *Uh-oh. What's this all about?* There was something else on his mind, but did he feel like sharing it? "Gimme one of those!" Boob said, eyeing a handful of small pink snack packs sticking out of Rube's pockets. *Guess that answers my question.* Each package was covered in joyful-seeming animals showered in corn and Japanese writing. Boob grabbed one, ripped it open, and poured its contents into his mouth.

"Enjoy it, my friend." Rube loved watching Boob devour his favorite foods. *Like being at the zoo.* "Sweet corn flavor. Nice mix of salt and spices. Solid crunch. These are the last few we've got until my dad goes to Japan again. It's our duty to savor every single bite."

CRUNCH! "This is the best thing I've eaten all week." *CRUNCH!*

"It's only Monday." Rube noticed a bruise on Boob's arm. "Hey, is that from this morning when you tripped?"

"Huh? Oh yeah."

The uncertain tone of Boob's voice made Rube curious. *There's something he's not telling me.* He bookmarked the detail for later. The boys lay down on the roof, gazing up at the stars in silence. Though neither of them kept his mouth shut for long.

"What do you see when you look up there?" Boob asked.

"Machines," Rube said without hesitation. "All their different parts." He pointed to a unique constellation. "Like that one right there? We've got a toucan, a window fan, and a sailboat in a bathtub. Throw in a couple more parts, and it's an easy way to toast a bagel!" He shifted his attention to a different star cluster. "That one is obviously a whisk, a folding tray table, and a wall clock with a swinging pendulum. A rig that brings us tasty little morsels!"

Boob squinted. He *really* wanted to see Rube's vision. "Uh, yeah. I see all that stuff too. The thing. And the other thing. It's, um, cool." All of a sudden, Boob turned away. He looked off in the middle distance. There was something on his mind that ached to be free. "I wish I knew where we're supposed to go when we're done here."

"You and I are moving to New York City after we graduate high school. We've already talked about this."

"No, I mean what happens to us when we die?"

The question made Rube feel a little uncomfortable, but he joked about it anyway. "Well, for starters, I'll replace ol' Gladys as the town ghost and torment everyone who ever did me wrong. The Cowboy Specter who rides at night! You can be my faithful sidekick, Haunty."

"Stop with the ghost stuff. I'm already freaked out as it is."

"Before my mom died, she said our bodies are like hermit crab shells. One day, our spirit outgrows our shell and moves into something bigger and better."

"Yeah, but *what?!*"

"That." His arms wide open, Rube presented the sky, in its entirety, to Boob. "Our bodies are made up of everything in the universe. Elements, minerals, it's all inside us. *We are the universe.* There's a theory that says the universe is conscious. It can feel stuff like a human, because it's aware of its existence."

"This is very confusing. How is any of that possible?"

"*I don't know*, Boob. How is *anything* possible?"

"Hey, remember when you won a hermit crab at the fair?"

"Sir Crabs-A-Lot was the best."

"Whatever happened to that thing?"

"It died."

"Great. Now every time I look up at the night sky, I'm going to think of Sir Crabs-A-Lot. But I guess it's better than worrying about asteroids hitting the Earth. *Which they might*."

"Sir Crabs-A-Lot is up there somewhere, along with everyone else." Rube noticed Boob zoning out. He couldn't tell if he was sad or sleepy. "Something on your mind, B?"

"Just thinking about homework 'n' stuff."

"Don't outgrow your hermit crab shell on me, okay? We've got a lot of stuff we have to accomplish. First, we conquer the planet. *Then* we conquer the universe. That's the rule."

Boob smiled. "I like when we do this."

"Me too." Rube sighed. "I think I have anxiety."

"Spider-Man has anxiety."

"He has cool powers, though."

"And he lives an exciting life in New York City," Boob said. "But one day, we'll be living an exciting life there too. *Hopefully*." Boob leaned his head on Rube's shoulder. "I think *your* powers are pretty cool. Even if you don't show 'em to me."

"Thanks, pal."

You know what? Life is good.

CHAPTER 5

"Looking nice, looking nice . . ."

After a few weeks of trial and error, things were looking up for ol' Rube Goldberg. Not only was he worrying less, but now he was getting a whole six hours of sleep a night. Little victories were still victories. Not that he was winning across the board, though. School took a back seat to machine making. Rube failed to turn in two reports and bombed a few quizzes. His teachers warned him that he had to step up his game, but that could come later. Con-Con came first. Once it was over, he'd pick up the slack and go above and beyond to get his grades where they needed to be. A few Fs mixed with a few As equal a few Cs, which was all he needed to pass. And if that didn't work?

It will.

"Almost finished . . ."

The Science Lab was not for machine building, but Rube's house had become unbelievably cluttered and he felt the need

to switch things up. Twice a week, during Study Hall, he'd slip in and mess around for a bit when the room wasn't occupied. After a rigorous screening process, he whittled down the Con-Con contenders so only a select few remained. There were failures along the way, some more heartbreaking than others. But Rube tried his hardest to focus on successes like the Nose Picker, which had become a beloved front-runner with endless comedic potential. *My favorite kind of potential.* The premise was simple—picking your nose is gross. Why not build something that picked it for you? *Pure genius.*

"This should do the trick!"

After Rube switched a few parts out, the Nose Picker was finally ready for a trial run. It had winner written all over it. Rube set the machine in motion, watching each step execute perfectly. It worked better than he expected. So much better that the machine's grand finale, *the Pickening*, was fast approaching. Can't have a Nose Picker without a nose to pick. Rube raced to get in place for the grand finale, but before he made it, Mr. Blank swung open the door to the Science Lab unexpectedly.

"*Gah!*"

Startled by his sudden appearance, Rube tripped and fell into the Nose Picker, almost demolishing the machine completely. Had this happened at home, Rube might consider it a small setback

(albeit still an embarrassing one). However, failing in front of the person who helps decide the winner of Con-Con was a different story. He'd just eaten a heaping helping of humiliation with a side of all-consuming frustration. Rube wanted to scream at the top of his lungs. Thankfully, he didn't. That would have been bad.

"The Science Lab is not the place for experimentation," sneered Mr. Blank. "You were warned about this."

That doesn't make any sense!

Mr. Blank was one of the new teachers at Beechwood, and little was known about him aside from the fact that he didn't seem to be a happy guy. Rube was fascinated with his black, helmetlike hair. "Vader-esque" was the word he used. Even Mr. Blank's wrinkles were strange. It was as if someone blew him up like a balloon and stretched his skin as far as it could go. Then, as he deflated, his loose skin was draped over a skeleton and topped off with a pair of dark glasses. Mr. Blank surveyed the remains of Rube's machine, using his index finger to move its parts around, looking for flaws. "What was the name of this . . . masterpiece?" His voice dripped with snark.

"The Nose Picker."

"How *innovative*," Mr. Blank said, rolling his eyes. "Clean up this mess and leave."

Instead of explaining himself and saying things he might regret later, Rube got to work picking up the machine's broken pieces. Mr. Blank sat down at his desk and watched Rube like a hawk. It was deeply uncomfortable. The whole room simmered in tension. It was too much for Rube to bear. Awkward conversation was on the menu.

"How do you like Beechwood so far?" he asked.

"It's fine."

Mr. Blank's hair shimmered in the sunlight. It looked as if it was hard as a rock. Rube couldn't stop staring. "Do you use product in your hair? I do sometimes. My hair gets frizzy. Does yours ever get frizzy? There's this oil my dad got in Morocco—he travels a lot for work—that's really good for frizzy hair. You should check it out." Mr. Blank's glare was cold and confused. "I'm just nervous about Con-Con. I really want to make something cool that will blow everyone else's machines out of the water. *Respectfully*."

"First you have to make something that *functions*," replied Mr. Blank, flashing a fake smile. "Then you can worry about accolades and acclaim."

"You sound like Professor Butts," Rube muttered under his breath.

Mr. Blank's left eyebrow raised. "What did you just say?"

"Oh, um, nothing. There's this guy that lives in my neighborhood." Rube quickened his pace, shoving pieces of the Nose Picker into his pockets. "I wasn't calling *you* a bad name or anything. Please don't get me in trouble."

Mr. Blank took his glasses off and laid them on his desk. "You know, Rube, passion is no substitute for commitment. Consider that you may not be cut out for this competition. Perhaps it would behoove you to focus your energy on something you're actually *good* at doing. Just a thought."

The words hit Rube like a ton of bricks. His stomach started churning. His hands turned damp and clammy. He had to get out of there. "Thanks for the pep talk." He grabbed his backpack and headed out. Rube wasn't sure what exactly was happening inside him, but he wasn't about to risk an accident. He ducked into the boy's restroom, splashed water on his face, and tried to calm down. "You got this, Goldberg," he told his reflection in the mirror. "Con-Con is still a couple weeks away. You've got plenty of time to figure things out. Dry your face, get your head in the game, and handle your business."

"Ruuuuuube?"

A somber voice called out from one of the side stalls. Rube turned to see who it was, his face dripping wet, but he didn't spot any legs dangling. *Am I going crazy? Or was Boob actually right?! Are there really ghosts around here!?* The sound of heavy breathing was definitely coming from the side. *No smell. That's a good sign.* He walked over, carefully opening the first, then the second door, and found Boob crouched on top of the toilet seat. "What the fuzz are you doing!?"

"Oh, you know, just hanging out."

Before Rube could properly interrogate Boob on his odd behavior, Mike and Ike burst into the restroom, pushing each other around like a couple of drunken monkeys. Rube slammed the stall door shut, returned to the sink, and pretended everything was fine. "Good afternoon, gentlemen," he said. "Nice day for a pee." *Stop talking, Rube!*

"Hahaha." Ike pointed at Rube. "I bet *you* just pooped."

Rube smirked. "Everyone does. It's not a big deal."

Mike began kicking open the bathroom stall doors, one by one. He clutched his phone tightly, recording whatever he found inside. But he wasn't stuffing the toilets with paper or writing graffiti on the walls. *He's looking for someone.* Rube ran interference.

"Have you smelled this?" he asked, presenting the out-of-date soap dispenser. "Mint *and* cucumber. Two powerful titans, coming together to create a fragrance unlike anything the world has ever smelled before. Who knew?"

"Shut *up*, Goldberg," Ike grumbled.

Mike reached the corner stall. *Uh-oh, Boob's in trouble.* He tried kicking the locked door open, hurting his foot in the process. That made him extra mad. Inside the stall, Boob stayed quiet as a mouse. *Do not open your mouth.* Mike craned his head down to look for feet but didn't see any. Agitated by the lack of closure, he turned his attention to Rube.

"What are you even doing in here anyway?" asked Mike.

"Practicing my dance moves, of course." Rube wiggled and shook his body as awkwardly as he possibly could. It was an old trick he used to make bullies uncomfortable. That way, they wouldn't know how to react and just walk away. Based on Mike's and Ike's disgusted expressions, the plan was working.

FLUSH!

Then Boob accidentally flushed the toilet in his stall.

It was like a vortex of water being summoned forth by an old god. Rube panicked. "Look over there!" he shouted, pointing to the stall at the opposite end. "It's the Phantom Pooper!" Mike and Ike scurried over to check it out. As they stuck their heads in to investigate, Boob escaped out the door. Rube followed closely behind. "Oops. False alarm. Bye!" They hid in a janitor's closet nearby until Mike and Ike cleared the scene. Once it was safe to come out, they conferred in the hallway, where Rube had a few pressing questions for Boob.

"What was that all about!? Were Mike and Ike looking for you?"

"Not *exactly*," Boob said. "I think they just wanted to talk to someone."

Rube gripped Boob by the shoulders and looked him square in the face. "If either of those two caveboys give you a hard time, you have to tell me. Promise?" His tone was deadly serious.

"Yeah," Boob said, his eyes cast downward.

"Say it."

"*I promise*." He slipped out of Rube's grasp and suggested a different option. "What if you made a machine that embarrassed them in front of the entire school? Something that involves diapers and them wetting their pants, maybe?"

Before Rube could respond to Boob's odd request, a familiar face came gliding down the hall to greet them. "Well, well, well," Pearl said with a smile. "My old friends hanging out without me once again. If I knew any better, I might think this was a conspiracy."

"Too bad you're never around long enough to find out. What with all of your activities and such." *That was a little harsh.*

More than anything, Pearl was amused by Rube's pointed remark. She had no shame in having a busy schedule. "Principal Kim wants to see you."

"*Funny*," Rube replied.

"I'm serious," Pearl said. "Last week, he made me his office assistant. Not only that, I'm also running for sixth-grade class president. Why don't you guys come over tonight and help me make flyers and stuff? My brother has a button maker. It'll be fun."

Boob burst with joy. "Buttons! I want to make buttons!" Then he remembered something. "But I can't tonight. I've got a date with the Internet. Ghost business."

"Boob, c'mon," Rube said. "That ghost thing is so silly."

"No, it's not. An evil spirit has been awakened. We have to be prepared."

"Where's that doll?" Pearl asked.

"*Gladys* is resting in my locker," Boob replied. "There's no way I'm taking that thing home with me. I'll spread the curse! I gotta get back to class. Save some buttons for me!"

Boob took off down the hallway, leaving Rube to contemplate Pearl's offer. She could smell the cageyness before he even opened his mouth. "Just say it, Goldberg."

"I *would*, but I'm . . ."

"Working on a machine. Same story you've been giving me for weeks. When do I get an invitation to come see these amazing contraptions?"

"World-class chefs don't invite people into their kitchen to show them how they make their most famous dishes." *Good analogy, Rube.*

"But *you've* only been 'cooking' since this summer. Nice try, though."

She has a point. "You got me there." Rube wanted to come out swinging and rise to the top on the first day. But that's not how things worked.

Pearl checked her watch. "I've got to go grab some paperwork about setting up a new STEM program. ♫ Exciting! ♫ You need to go see Principal Kim. We'll link up later."

Rube shuffled down the hall to Principal Kim's office. Miss Mary ushered him in. "He's been expecting you," she said. "Good luck!"

Good luck?! What does that mean?

Principal Kim was looking at his phone. "Rube!" he exclaimed, fumbling the device as he turned it off. "Glad you're here."

Rube planted his butt and got down to business. "If this is about what happened with Mike and Ike just now, Boob and I were only making jokes. I would never build a Diaper-Changing Machine to embarrass them in front of the whole school. I don't even know if they wear diapers! But they *are* giant babies, so it makes sense—"

"*Stop.* Diaper-changing . . . ? No, that's not what I'm talking about."

"Oh. I thought . . . um . . . never mind."

"What have you heard about this ghost stuff?"

Uh-oh. "What . . . ghost . . . stuff?" Rube played dumb better than most people. Or, at least, he *thought* he did.

"There have been strange occurrences around here. Some of the staff reported odd sounds coming from the boiler room. Lights flickering off and on after hours. Items have gone missing." Principal Kim leaned in, speaking in hushed tones. "Beechwood has a history of supernatural incidents. We don't want students to be frightened, of course. You're not in any danger. But if the local news calls, put them in touch with me, would you?"

Boob was right. Rube gulped. "Yes sir," he said, getting ready leave.

"Wait. That's not why I called you in." Principal Kim leaned back in his chair. "Rube, you're a gifted student. I noticed it back when you were in elementary school. Artistic. Technical. A clever mind like yours is a blessing. I know sometimes it might feel like a curse."

"Get on with it," Rube said flatly. "Sorry. I mean, um, *go on*."

"There's that short fuse I remember." *Quit stalling.* "Your teachers have told me you haven't been completing assignments, and you're already failing two classes."

"It's only the beginning of the school year. If I ace everything in the second part of the semester, I could make a B average, assuming I do all the extra credit."

"That's not a workable approach."

Bad news is coming. Rube felt it in his bones.

"There are academic qualifications for the Contraption Convention, Rube. And I'm afraid you haven't met them. Mr. Blank and I are very sorry, but you're no longer allowed to compete."

CHAPTER 6

"Excuse me?!" Rube hollered. His hands were shaking. He wasn't sure if he was going to cry or throw up. "Are you *serious* right now!?"

Delivering bad news wasn't easy for Principal Kim. It broke his heart to remove Rube from the competition. But he had a job to do, regardless of the circumstances. "These are the rules," he said calmly. "Rube, I wish there was something I could do—"

"You're the dang principal! You can do anything you want!" *Don't, Rube.* He began pacing around the room, trying to expel his nervous energy.

"Please understand, you're not alone. Other underperforming students have been removed from the competition as well."

"But I'm the only one that *cares*." Rube stopped moving and gave all of his attention to the man in charge. "Con-Con isn't just some fun after-school activity, Principal Kim. It's what I've been waiting for. *It's everything to me.* You can't take it away. *Please.* I'm begging you."

Principal Kim could see from the tears welling in Rube's eyes that the boy was speaking his truth as best he could. "I think we should call your father."

"Good luck with that," Rube said. "He's away on business. He's *always* away on business. And even if he wasn't, he wouldn't waste his time coming in here to talk to the manager of Taco Cavern. Oh wait. I'm sorry. *Assistant* manager."

Whoa. That was inappropriate. And uncalled-for.

"That was inappropriate and uncalled-for," Principal Kim said. "You just earned yourself a detention."

Rube kicked a chair in anger but got his shin entangled in the chair leg. As he tried to shake himself free, he tripped and fell right on his butt. "I'm *fine*." Principal Kim tried to help Rube up but was pushed away.

BRRRRRRRRRING!

"Let's get this over with." Rube grabbed his backpack and stormed out of the office, huffing, puffing, and not paying attention. As he rounded a corner, he ran smack dab into Mr. Blank. "Excuse me," Rube muttered in a low tone. "I've got to get to detention."

"I'm heartbroken to hear that," said Mr. Blank.

"I'm sure," Rube replied. *You can shove your fake apology.* He didn't want to hear it. Instead of doing what he was meant to be doing, Rube was stuck serving time in a student prison. *Two hours' worth of nothing?* He walked into detention slowly, as if marching to his death. *What a complete waste of time.* He parked himself in the back corner next to the only other detainee, who was passed out cold with his head down on the desk.

Mr. Badalucco, the world history teacher, waddled in and flopped into his seat. His tight suit hugged his stout body, turning his sun-kissed face an even brighter bright red. He looked like a strangled tomato. *That guy is gonna pop any second now.* His dark, slicked-back hair revealed stark gray roots. Years ago, a student told him his beard was legendary, so he never shaved it again. Outside of being legendarily thick, it also smelled. Mr. Badalucco had a reputation for sneaking sips of energy drinks in class. He'd pour cans of the stuff into his thermos and drink from it all day long. Word around school was they made him a little bonkers. "No sleeping!" he shouted, slamming his hand down on the desk.

The guy next to Rube suddenly sprung to life, wiping his eyes and yawning. A dark hoodie obscured his face. *What's this kid all about?* Rube intentionally dropped his pencil on the ground and watched it roll behind him. He reached to pick it up, getting a better look at his fellow detainee. The boy was tired for sure, but he also looked sad. Not that detention was supposed to be a ball of joy or anything. *Where do I know him from?* Rube wracked his brain until an epiphany slapped him in the face. *Aha! The kid with the black bangs!* Rube hadn't seen him since the first week of school.

"No phones. No food. No music. No talking. No horseplay."
Mr. Badalucco looked up at the clock on the side of the wall. "Settle
in, boys. We've got two hours together. Let's hope it goes as quick
as possible." He smoothed a newspaper out on the desk in front of
him and began to read. Thirty seconds later, he was asleep. The
energy drink crash was real.

Rube got out his notebook and doodled while the other boy
stared at him, watching every pencil stroke. *What's up with this
kid?* Having his movements studied made Rube uncomfortable, so
he turned around and made eye contact with the boy. It was a little
trick he learned back when he took a self-defense class. Direct eye
contact let an attacker know you were not to be messed with.

The boy backed off. "Sorry. Didn't mean to stare like a creeper.
You draw really well."

"Thanks," Rube said.

"Self-taught?"

"Yeah. Mostly. There are some good videos online if you want
to learn technique."

"Cool. Thanks. I'm Zach."

"Rube."

"I'm a lefty too, by the way." He pointed to Mr. Badalucco, who
was snoring like a freight train. "We should just leave. He'd never
know."

"Nah," Rube said, shaking his head. "The door is way too creaky. He'd hear it open and wake up immediately."

"So? If we ran, there's no way he'd catch us."

"But he *would* report us for skipping. We'd get stuck in here again or, worse, suspended. Then again, it might be worth it just to watch him try to run. Poor guy might explode." That made Zach laugh. "Welcome to Beechwood. What brought you to this paradise?"

"My dad's job. We move around a lot. It's the worst. But I don't have a mom I can stay with, so there's nothing I can do about it."

"I don't have a mom either!" Rube exclaimed. "Well, I mean, I *did*, but she died." *What are you saying right now?!* "Yikes. That sounds dark. I just meant . . ." He struggled to finish his thought but couldn't make it happen. "I'll shut up now."

"It's okay, man. Sorry about your mom. And dark is cool with me."

It had been a long while since Rube brought up his mom with anyone other than his dad, Boob, or Pearl. It felt strange. But good. Now that his mom was on his mind, he wanted to tell Zach all the reasons why she was awesome, but he also didn't want Zach to think he was weird.

"You play video games?" Zach asked.

"Yeah, sometimes," Rube replied. "But after I conquered Gareth of the Crystalverse, I kind of lost interest. It was way too predictable."

"I code. And make websites," Zach said, shifting in his seat. "Might try to build my own gaming system one of these days."

Suddenly, Zach swiped Rube's notebook out from under him. "What the fuzz?!" he exclaimed.

"Shhhh. You'll wake up Badalucco." Zach flipped through the journal, looking over Rube's doodles and designs. "What's the Jiggler?"

None of your business. "It helps you put a shirt on." Irritated by the invasion of privacy, Rube reached across the aisle and snatched his notebook back, almost falling out of his desk as he reached for it.

"Cool," Zach said.

What game is this kid playing? "I was going to make a machine for Con-Con, but then I got kicked out. It's partly why I'm stuck in detention. What are *you* in for?"

"Don't worry about it." Zach grinned. "You into science?"

"Yeah. I read scientific journals sometimes. They can be hard to understand, but they make sense to me."

"Hey, me too. My dad makes me read them. At first, they were *so boring*, but after a while, they actually turned out to be really cool. There was this one article about scientists in California who discovered a way to upload information directly into the human brain. It's still experimental. But just think *no more studying.* All we'd have to do is put some crazy helmet on if we wanted to learn something."

Without thinking, Rube began jotting down notes and sketching a new machine. It was like he'd fallen into a trance. *Gotta ride this wave.* He was in the zone again and loving it. Zach watched him like a hawk. It was hard not to. Rube had impressive speed and skill. From the look of it, he was designing a piece of headgear attached to a mechanical apparatus. His line work was exceptional. But the more he drew, the more frustrated he became. Where would he debut any of his work? *At home? The park?* Con-Con was a complete bust. *What's the point!?!?* Disappointed and hurt, he stopped himself from finishing, closed his notebook, and put it aside. There would be no more new machines.

"What if you built something that could get us out of here?" Zach suggested. *Now, why did you go and say that?* "There's a ton of stuff we could use for parts." He gestured toward a hamster cage that was labeled MORTIMER X. FUZZINGTON, CUDDLE KING OF BEECHWOOD.

Lightbulbs burst like fireworks inside Rube's head. *Okay, one more machine.* First, he had to think it through. "We'd need to push the clock hands ahead manually." He glanced around the room for usable parts. "We've got a curtain cord we could use as a pulley, a stapler that works as lever, and a desk that serves as a plane. It's a good start, I guess. But we'd have to set everything up very quietly, then give ourselves time to disassemble the machine and put everything back where it belongs before the clock hits 4:30 P.M. Once *that* happens, we wake him up."

"Or we could just use the ladder and move the clock hands ourselves."

He's got a point. "Yeah but where's the fun in that?" Rube's mischievous grin gave way to unbridled excitement. *Be aware that you're about to cheat yourself out of detention, Rueben.* "Yes, I know that!"

"Who are you talking to?"

"No one. *Let's do this.*" Just like that, they were off to the races. Zach tiptoed through the room, gathering usable parts while Rube sketched out an idea. Before today, neither of them had ever worked with another person to build a machine. Rube usually made them alone in his room, without the aid of his friends. But if he wanted to execute this particular mission, teamwork was the only option. *If that's how it has to be, that's how it has to be.* After a rough sketch was completed, assembly began. While Rube constructed the machine, Zach double-checked each step in the notebook, sneaking peeks at its other pages along the way. Rube gingerly put Mortimer X. Fuzzington's cage into position. *Don't let us down, little guy.* In a matter of minutes, their masterpiece had come together. It was a glorious sight to behold. And just a wee bit wobbly.

"What do we call it?" Zach asked.

"What else? *The Time Machine,*" replied Rube.

No time for a test run. It was *now* or never. Rube set the device in motion, proudly watching each step execute perfectly. It all came down to Mortimer X. Fuzzington. The cheerful little hamster hopped onto his wheel, running as fast as he could. CLICK! The

masterstroke had been delivered. The mission completed in record time. Everything had gone exactly according to plan. Now came the hard part. Rube and Zach had only two minutes to disassemble the device and sit back down. But they got it done in one.

"Mr. Badalucco!" Rube shouted.

"Don't hurt me! I'll be a good boy!" Mr. Badalucco cried out. He patted himself down to make sure he was safe. "Oops. Must've dozed off. Has anyone seen my thermos?"

Zach pointed at the clock. "Time to go."

Mr. Badalucco yawned. "All righty, then. Get outta here, you two," he said with a smirk. "And thanks for behaving. Makes my job that much easier."

Rube and Zach calmly picked up their things and sauntered out of the room. *No celebrating till we're outside.* They swung open the front door of the school and released a howl of excitement.

"That was amazing!" Zach said. "He had *no idea.*"

"None! No clue whatsoever!"

The boys took their time strolling over to the bike rack, savoring the moment of their freedom with every step. *We actually did it.* Rube wasn't keen on making new friends and hadn't expected to find a kindred spirit in Zach. But he couldn't deny it—the kid knew what he was doing.

"There's this new virtual reality game at Party Palace USA

where you sit in some egg thing and eat cupcakes while fighting off giant vampire chinchillas. Wanna go?" asked Zach.

"Riding your bike all the way downtown is dangerous," Rube said, contemplating the offer. "Don't you have to cross the highway?"

"Yeah. I do it all the time. Is that a problem?"

Boob appeared from behind a nearby tree. "You told Pearl you were working on a machine tonight." His sudden presence surprised and disturbed Rube. *Is he spying on me?*

"I know what I told Pearl," he replied. "But things have changed."

Zach's phone vibrated. "Be right back," he said, walking away to take the call.

"That's Zach," Rube said. "He's new in town."

"Cool." Boob's voice was shyer than usual. "Hey, I picked up *Godzilla vs. Mechagodzilla* from the library today. If you're free tonight, we should watch it over at Pearl's while we help her get her campaign stuff together."

Normally, Rube would never turn down a chance to watch one of his all-time favorites with his best friend. But tonight, he wasn't feeling it. "First of all, we've seen *Godzilla vs. Mechagodzilla* a million times. Second of all, aren't you doing your stupid ghost investigation? How can you do that *and* help Pearl?" *Ouch, Rube. Didn't mean for that to come out so rude.*

"It's not *stupid*." Boob wasn't having any of Rube's attitude. "And I'm good at multitasking. Also, I saw your shady new friend steal string cheese from the lunch counter a few weeks ago. Slipped 'em into his pocket when he thought no one was looking."

"You didn't see anything. Cut it out and stop being judgy."

Zach had finished his phone call and jumped on his bike. "You ready?"

Rube wasn't sure. Zach seemed like a chill guy, but Boob was his best friend. *Why do I have to make a choice here? I just want to do what I want to do. What's the issue?*

"If Pearl is going to win, she's needs our help."

Zach chuckled. "No offense, but student government is

lame. It's all show. The titles are fake. Nobody cares. Twelve- and thirteen-year-olds can't actually *do* anything."

"*Pearl* cares. *Pearl* is gonna do something."

"Sure, man. Keep believing that," Zach replied.

All of a sudden, Boob's face warped. His nose started crinkling as his eyes grew wider and wider. *Don't do it. Don't you do it.* "AHHHHH-CHOO!" Boob turned and sneezed in Zach's direction, showering him with a light coating of mucus.

"Ugh! Cover your mouth when you sneeze!" Zach bellowed.

"Sorry," Boob said, with a sly, understated smirk. He handed

Zach a few tissues. "I have allergies."

Zach wiped his face, discarding the gooey tissues on the ground. "I'm taking off."

"I'm coming with you," said Rube.

"So what am *I* supposed to do?" Boob shrugged.

"*I don't know, Boob.*" Rube threw his hands up. "Do you want to come with us?"

Zach cringed. "No offense but . . ." He stopped short of saying something mean, but his body language had done all the talking for him. Boob *wasn't* welcome.

"Pearl needs me," said Boob. "But thanks anyway."

"Go to Pearl, then, and stop being annoying," Rube replied, immediately flustered by his poor choice of words. "You know what I mean."

"Actually, I don't." Boob crossed his arms, unabashedly smirking. "Why don't you explain yourself so we're crystal clear?"

Okay, now you're really getting on my nerves. "Find another friend, Boob. Just one," Rube snapped. "So I don't have to do the heavy lifting all the time." He and Boob glared at each other in silence. *That may have been the wrong thing to say . . .*

"*Dude,*" Zach pressed. "Are you done?"

"Oh yeah," Rube said. "I'm done." He and Zach took off on their bikes, headed downtown, leaving Boob all by himself.

CHAPTER 7

As the summer heat faded away, mornings became cooler. Rube rode to school by himself, earlier than usual, and hung around the bike racks waiting for Boob to arrive. The events of the previous day were still fresh in his mind. Generally, when the two of them had disagreements, they swept them under the rug. With a little distance and time, petty stuff was forgotten. No apology needed. Like the time they built a fort in Rube's basement during a sleepover. The roughhousing got out of hand. Words were used as weapons (along with a few ratty old pillows). When they woke up the next day, it all felt like a bad dream. Everything went right back to normal. Boob knew Rube was sorry. Rube knew Boob was sorry. Saying it out loud felt weird, so they never did. But now they were older. Feelings mattered in a brand-new way. And they weren't always easy to figure out. As Boob rolled up on his bike, the sour look on his face told Rube all he needed to know.

"How was Party Palace USA? Did you and Zeb eat boxes of

Sugar Strands and win mangy green teddy bears?" Boob asked. "I heard that place has bedbugs. Don't get close to me."

"We didn't go. I mean, *he* went. I went home to help my grandma. All *Zach* and I did was grab sodas, hang out in a gas station parking lot, and talk for a little while. Is that a crime?"

"Might be. Did you steal the sodas? It's a valid question, considering the company you're keeping nowadays."

The two boys stared at each other, annoyed by their own behavior. Middle school hormones didn't mix well with stubbornness. Rube wanted to tell Boob to mind his own business. *But that's not how you solve this problem.* Instead, he chose honesty.

"I was kicked out of Con-Con yesterday," Rube said softly.

The revelation took Boob's breath away. He was overcome with heartbreak for his friend, though he tried not to show it. When one hurt, so did the other. Rube and Boob were connected like that. Getting kicked out of Con-Con was a huge blow, and they both felt it. When Rube first talked about machine making, Boob knew it was more than just a hobby. His best friend had found his passion (even though he didn't want to share it with anyone). But Boob understood. There were things about himself that he didn't want to share either. "Why didn't you say anything?"

"I . . . just . . ." Rube stumbled. "It's embarrassing."

"Sure, but it's not the end of the world. What's the reason?"

"Apparently, my grades are bad."

"How is that possible? We *just* started school. There hasn't even been a big test yet."

"That's what I'm sayin'!" Rube exclaimed. "I think someone is out to get me."

"Let's set a trap! I've been working on a disguise kit. It's got makeup, costumes, the works. I've even been collecting chunks of hair to make a fake beard. I know how that sounds, but don't worry. It's dog hair. Top-of-the-line, not the cheap stuff."

"Gross."

"Did you tell that kid Zach that you were kicked out of Con-Con?"

He had to go and put me on the spot, didn't he? "Yeah."

"Huh." Boob nodded.

Before Rube could explain himself further, a sudden commotion erupted inside Beechwood Middle School as students spilled out of the hallways and onto the playground.

"Get it off of me!!!" a boy screamed, pushing through the throng. He took off running down the street at full speed. "Evil has come to Beechwood!"

"What . . . the . . . !?"

Rube and Boob raced inside to see what was up. They never imagined they'd find such a bizarre sight. The locker bay was coated in thick, neon orange slime. Oozing sludge dripped from the ceiling. Chunky puddles of muck were scattered everywhere. They smelled like rotten milk. Students slipped and tripped as they made their way through the area. Regan Winter got slime in her hair and couldn't stop crying. Logan Lucas ate a handful of goo and puked all over the drinking fountain. Teachers did their best to calm everyone, but their best wasn't good enough. Beechwood Middle School had been attacked, and from the looks of things, the prime suspect was supernatural.

"Demons ate my homework!" a girl shouted to no one in particular.

Principal Kim tried to console her but quickly became

overwhelmed. "Everyone needs to calm down!" he exclaimed. "And for the love of Pete, don't touch anything."

Boob pushed through the insanity to reach his locker, where an ominous surprise was waiting. "Gladys is gone," he panted breathlessly as he rummaged through his things. "I put her in here yesterday, and now she's gone!"

"Gladys?" Rube asked, distracted by everything around him.

"The creepy doll!" exclaimed Boob. As students freaked out around him, Boob calmly sat down on the ground to gather his thoughts. "We've unlocked something bad, Rube. Something really, *really* bad."

"What are you talking about?" Rube sat down next to Boob and gave him his full attention.

"One hundred years ago, there was a little girl named Gladys who disappeared in the woods near the Lair. She wandered away from her house to look for her dog and was never seen again. Years after she went missing, hunters said a little girl would appear to them. She was always glowing like she was on fire. And she was *always* holding her doll."

"Hold up. The creepy doll?"

"Yes, the creepy doll! It's the *only* doll in our lives right now! Unless you've still got that one weird Barbie with the shaved head and tattoos."

"I do, actually. Oooooo, maybe I could use her in a machine—"

"AHEM!"

"Sorry." Rube zipped his lip.

"The creepy doll contains Gladys's restless spirit. That thing is possessed, and I'm the one that brought it here. Don't you get it?! *I did this.* I left the doll in my locker overnight and now . . ."

Rube put a calming hand on Boob's shoulder. "That doesn't mean—"

"*We're cursed,*" Boob said bluntly. "The whole school is. Guess my investigation isn't as stupid as you thought."

Rube spotted Pearl at the far end of the hall and motioned for her to come over. *Help me out here, wouldja?* As she moved through the crowded, noisy hall, Pearl ran her hand across the slime-covered lockers. Samples needed collecting. "Hmmm. It's definitely gooey. Fluorescent orange is an interesting color. Light on the stickiness," she observed. "Warm, wet, and, *uuugggghhh,* chunky."

"It's ectoplasm," Boob said. He'd never been so sure in his life.

"Ectoplasm has no scientific basis," Pearl explained. "*This* stuff is very real. But it's not like what you'd buy at a toy store either. It's different. Homemade, maybe? Something strange is definitely going on around here."

Mike and Ike posted themselves near the drinking fountain,

taking photos on the sly as the action unfolded. Rumors swirled that the twins had stolen a set of keys that opened every single door in the school. It was hard to tell if they had anything to do with this particular incident, since everything they did was suspicious. But the trail of giant-sized slime footprints that ended mysteriously near the supply closet next to the drinking fountain certainly didn't do them any favors. They weren't the brightest boys in school, after all. Mike ran over to the school's newly slimed trophy case, stuck his tongue out, and took a selfie. A single drop of slime fell from the ceiling and into his mouth. "Blech!" he screeched, scraping his tongue with his fingers.

"Put that phone away!" yelled Principal Kim. "There are rules around here! You don't want to know what happens if I see that photo on social media tagged with #BeechwoodGhost!"

BRRRRRRRRRING!

Students scuttled to class as the janitorial staff began cleaning the lockers. Once the insanity died down, Principal Kim took a few photos of his own. "For evidence."

The ghost mystery had taken a serious turn. There was no denying it. Beechwood was clearly under siege, and Rube was ready to take action. Before the next bell rang, he pulled his friends together and made his pitch. "We need to meet after school at the Lair and figure this out."

Boob couldn't believe his ears. Neither could Pearl. But she was distracted at the moment. Davin Drake had just tapped her on the shoulder. "Don't mean to interrupt," he said. "I'm going to the library to work on our project. Meet you there?"

Pearl nodded. "Yep!"

"This whole slime thing is

crazy, right? Makes you wonder," Davin said, flashing his mega-watt smile. "Be safe, guys."

Pearl's eyes followed him as he walked away. *This guy.* Davin was too good to be true. A football team captain in the honor society who was also the lead tenor in the show choir. Worst of all, he was genuinely *nice.* Hardly anyone disliked him. Davin dressed well too. His style was ahead of the curve, especially for a small town like Beechwood. Even the miserable kids couldn't deny his crushability. Not that Rube was jealous, of course.

"Wow. He's tall. And handsome," Boob said. "Must have about three inches on you, Rube. Don't worry, though. Puberty is coming for all of us. I'm sure it'll hit you sooner or later."

"At least I don't dress like a jobless clown," Rube shot back. *A dig for a dig.* "So. The Lair. Who's in?"

Pearl bit her bottom lip. "I've got chess practice," she said. "But I can *try* to make it."

"I'm busy too," Boob replied. "Very busy. Lots of important things going on in my life. Dinner and whatnot. TV shows. Looking for *clown* jobs. You name it. But good luck! I'll light a candle for you both." He turned his back on his friends and marched away to class.

"What was *that* about?" Pearl asked.

"He's being weird," Rube said, completely brushing the question aside. "I'm sure chess won't take *that* long. It's just a game. Come to the Lair after you get done."

BRRRRRRRRRING!

"Maybe," Pearl replied, heading toward the library.

That's hopeful, I guess. One more bridge to mend. Rube made a beeline for Principal Kim, slipping in behind him as he entered his office. "Good morning, sir."

"Rube!" Principal Kim shouted. "What the devil are you doing? Do *not* sneak up on people when they're in crisis. Why aren't you in class?"

"I just wanted to apologize for my behavior yesterday. It wasn't right of me to lose my cool. I'm not usually that immature, but I've been kind of stressed out lately."

"Well, thank you, Rube. I accept and appreciate your apology."

"You're welcome, sir. And I was just wondering . . ." *Here goes nothing.* "Is there *any* way you might let me back into Con-Con? I'm happy to do chores around the office. I'm *really* good at sorting colored pencils."

Principal Kim took his glasses off and massaged the skin between his eyes. "Rube," he said, squinting. "Disqualifying students makes me sad. You have *so much* potential. But rules are in place for reasons, and because of those reasons, we must adhere to them. I'm afraid there's nothing I can do."

"Let me show you something really quick." Rube zipped behind Principal Kim's desk and began rearranging the shelves of his bookcase. He moved all the knickknacks and books into a completely new configuration. Principal Kim was too tired to stop him. "Voilà! It's a simple machine. Don't have a name for it yet. Want to see how it works?"

CLAP . . . CLAP . . . CLAP . . .

"*Bravo*, Rueben." Mr. Blank had been watching from the office doorway. "That's quite a talent you have. It would be a shame not to share it with our school."

"That's what *I'm* saying."

"It's time we reinstated you into the Contraption Convention," declared Mr. Blank.

Principal Kim wasn't having it. "Now, hold on just a minute. That's not how things work around here. Rube is talented, yes. And it *is* a shame he can't participate. But if students or, God forbid, *parents* found out that we allowed this, it would be very, *very* bad."

"We'll say there was a mistake. It's a simple fix." Mr. Blank grinned. "Can you keep a secret, Principal Kim? I know *I* certainly can." A single droplet of sweat ran down Principal Kim's forehead. It cascaded across his nose and dripped onto the floor.

"If you feel that Rube deserves to be in the competition, then he's in the competition," he said, nervously. "The local news will

be here shortly to cover the slime incident. I need a few minutes to prepare myself, if you don't mind."

"Are there any leads yet?" Rube asked. "I saw Mike and Ike taking photos and being their jerkwad selves. They might be involved somehow."

Principal Kim bristled. "I'm handling the situation. Thank you, Rube. Rest assured, we'll get to the bottom of this mystery. Now run along to class, please."

"Let's leave our dear leader to his duties, shall we?" Mr. Blank escorted Rube out into the hallway. "You've been given an opportunity, Rueben. *Do better.*"

"Thank you so much, sir." Rube clutched Mr. Blank's hand and yanked it awkwardly. "I won't let you down!"

Zach turned the corner and was surprised to see Rube so happy. Especially after his defeat the day before. "What's going on?" he asked.

Mr. Blank slipped out of Rube's handshake. He reached into his pocket, pulled out sanitizer, and squirted some onto his palms. "I've reinstated Rube's participation in Con-Con," he said, cracking his knuckles. "It seems we made an unfortunate error that has since been corrected."

"I'm back in the game!" Rube cheered.

"You'll have to work hard to make sure he doesn't outshine

you, Zachary," Mr. Blank said with an eerie wink. "Good luck to the both of you."

As Mr. Blank sauntered down the hallway toward his classroom, Rube once again pondered his epic hairstyle. "How long do you think it takes him to get that look? Two hours? Three? I bet he sleeps in some weird coffin chamber."

"It's a wig."

"You think? But it's so *shiny*. Anyway, that guy is my new idol."

"He's a jerk," Zach scoffed. "Just wait till you have him for class."

"His handshake *was* like a limp fish. But who cares? I'm back, baby! And I've got all kinds of new ideas." Rube put his arm around Zach's shoulder. "Which reminds me. You never even told me what you were making for Con-Con."

"I'm still working it out. Want to get together after school and tackle our machines? My dad won't be home. We can do whatever we want."

"Perfect," said Rube.

Con-Con was two weeks away, but time was running out. Rube spent the rest of the day distractedly doodling in all of his classes. Every room he entered presented a world of new opportunities. *Maybe I could use Mrs. Fender's fish tank in a pancake-making machine? The hanging plants in the Science Room have big leaves. They might work nicely in a hair-drying machine. Ahhhhh, decisions, decisions, decisions.* His studies barely kept his attention. Not that anyone noticed. All people wanted to do was talk about the slime incident.

Everyone had a theory, including the lunch ladies. They weren't usually the superstitious type, but Hildegard (she handles the macaroni) said she felt a strange presence in the area. When the police came to investigate, another problem arose. The school's cameras had mysteriously glitched. Even if it was just a dumb prank, there was no way to find out the culprit. *Besides, it was probably just Mike and Ike being jerkwads.* By the end of the day, Rube had forgotten about the whole thing. He had other things to think about now that he had purpose again. After school, he headed toward Zach's house, but a nagging feeling made him change course midway. If Pearl showed up to the Lair and Rube wasn't there, she'd never forgive him. So he did what he had to do and went to the Lair. *Zach would understand.* Once Rube got there, he sketched to pass the time. After an hour or so, he'd designed a brand-new clubhouse complete with all kinds of machinery. Still no Pearl. *Chess probably isn't over yet.* Two hours later, Pearl still hadn't appeared. With a broken heart and a notebook full of new ideas, Rube packed up his stuff and went home. *Oh well. I tried.*

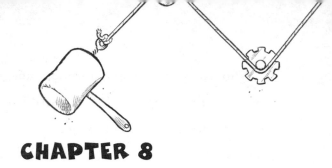

CHAPTER 8

"C'mon, you stupid thing!" Rube shouted. Bertha whimpered in the corner. "Not *you*, girl. You're fine. It's this stupid, freakin' machine that's the problem."

With Con-Con fast approaching, Rube had fallen into his old summer patterns. *Sleep? What's that?* The only thing that mattered was the doing. Even though he still didn't know what kind of machine he wanted to make. Would he indulge his fantasies or go for something practical? What about something bizarre and shocking? He had to create something spectacular that would WOW the crowd, but the selection process had drained him. Rube's faith was in the process of dying.

Why won't you work!?

With his dad still away on business, the whole house had become Rube's workshop and trash receptacle. Empty potato chip bags littered the couch. Machine parts were spread out across the floor in small piles. There were science journals, comic books, and microwave dinner bowls piled high on the coffee table. The place was certifiably filthy. Rube had successfully kept Grandma Etta away by visiting her twice a day instead of the other way around. *If she only knew.* As for Rube's friends, only Zach had been over. They'd become builder buddies, sharing tips and helping each other work out various machine-related issues. Zach was sharp and had a knack for locating weak points. When it came to his own machines, Zach kept his cards close to his vest. *I get it. He's insecure. He'll share the good stuff with me when the time is right.* In the interim, Rube did his best to encourage Zach, sharing ideas and helping him come up with solutions to whatever problems he mentioned he was having. Zach didn't talk much about personal stuff. He mostly focused on whatever Rube was doing. *What can I say? It feels nice to be admired.* But there was something brewing with Zach back at home. His father was being extra hard on him about something. Rube wasn't exactly sure of the situation and didn't push Zach to talk about it. Building stuff kept their minds occupied, though neither of them had settled on what to make for Con-Con.

What if I try something new . . . ?

Boob kept his distance from Rube, both socially and at school.

They made small talk, but that was it. Zach's presence had driven a strange wedge into their friendship. All of a sudden, he was everywhere, glued to Rube like they were old pals. At first, Boob chalked it up to "the machine thing." Zach and Rube had something unique in common. Can't get mad at that. But there were things about Zach that *really* irked Boob. Like the way he fake-smiled whenever Boob told a good joke. The stealing was a big issue, of course, but the way Zach always whispered in Rube's ear *really* got on Boob's nerves. It didn't matter what he was whispering about. It was obvious to Boob that the only reason Zach was doing it was to get under his skin. Mission accomplished. In addition to Boob generally feeling left out of the loop, he also hadn't been invited over to Rube's house in a long while. Mostly he hung out at the Lair by himself, trying to repair some of its weaker bits. Which wasn't so easy, since he had no clue what he was doing and didn't feel like asking for help. As for Rube, he didn't worry about his friendship with Boob one bit. Sure, he sensed things were a little off, but they'd been through stuff like this before. Once Con-Con was over, everything would bounce right back to normal. *Why wouldn't it?* They were bonded for life. A petty disagreement wasn't going to keep them apart. Boob wasn't so sure about that.

What can I do to fix you?

DING-DONG!

A surprise guest had arrived, and Bertha's ears were perky. The poor girl desperately needed a break from Rube's endless stress spiral. Whenever Zach came over, Bertha hid herself in the closet. But now her senses told her she was in for a good time. She raced through the house, doing circles in the living room. Anyone—but Zach—could've walked in and she'd be happy. That included the mail carrier, who she despised. But when Rube opened the door, she was extra excited to see the person on the other side.

"Hey," Pearl said, skateboard in hand. "Can I come in?"

Bertha leaped onto Pearl and gave her a boisterous welcome.

She licked, barked, and panted her way into Pearl's heart, just like she always did. It made Rube a little jealous.

"*Upstairs*," he commanded. Bertha followed orders, whimpering up to her dog bed on the second floor. Pearl took her helmet off and sat it on top of her skateboard as Rube waved her inside with the energy of a sleepy toddler.

"Whoa," Pearl said, stepping over a pile of parts. "I'm loving the mad scientist's work space thing you've got going on. Your dad will *really* enjoy coming home to *this*."

It was good to see his friend, but Rube *really* wasn't in the mood for sarcasm. "Why are you here?" he asked, scratching his head.

"I came by to see if you needed anything like, you know, friendship. Since you've been avoiding me and Boob, I thought some company might lighten your mood. We've started calling you *Rube-i-corn*, since you're a legendary creature rarely seen in the wild," Pearl said, taking a seat. "I came up with that. Pretty proud of it."

"It's funny. You should be."

"What if we got you out of your feelings and out of this house?"

Rube refused to sit down. "You've been avoiding me too. *Just so you know*. I'm surprised you found time to stop by, what with the Chess Team and Library Squad and, I don't know, *Plant Patrol*."

"Fine. *You got me*. I'm involved in a lot of extracurricular activities. But unlike you, I make time for my friends. Why don't we walk

down to Main Street and grab a cookie from Kandi's Crunchateria? Some nice, warm chocolate chips sound good, right? My mom gave me a gift card, so we can get as much as we want."

"I can't. Zach might be coming over."

"So, your new pal Zach gets to be on your team but your best friends don't?"

"We're *not* a team. He's been helping me. I've been helping him."

"Sounds like a team to me, but what do I know?" asked Pearl. "What else is new with you?"

That's a loaded question. Rube wanted to tell her all the thoughts that were swimming around in his head, but he could barely sort them out most days. He'd become so focused on his goal that it didn't matter if everything fell apart around him. *Keep your eyes on the prize.* He'd been waking up in the middle of the night, his heart beating out of his chest, unable to breathe. Waves of anxiousness kept him constantly on edge. He was starting to feel trapped again, like he did over the summer. But he couldn't say any of that to Pearl. *What good would it do?* Sharing his fears and insecurities might alienate her, and he wasn't about to risk that happening. *What are you even talking about? You've already alienated her! Have you been listening to a word she said? Just suck it up and tell her the truth.* Rube had become really good at mentally backing himself into a corner with no means of escape.

Any path he chose had its dangers. But *he* was the one who laid all the traps. Now he'd been presented an opportunity to come clean, which made him even *more* nervous. Making the wrong choice, revealing too much, could upend *everything. Okay, now you're being way overdramatic.* Though Pearl was a good friend *and* a superb listener, he just wasn't sure he was ready to pull the trigger. Once he started talking, he knew he wouldn't be able to stop. Explaining to Pearl that his affection for her had grown in a way he was still struggling to figure out? That was confusing enough for *him.* Telling *her* could be the thing that pushed her away completely. Ah. *Yeah, that would be really bad, now that I think about it.* Better to put up a shield and pretend like everything was A-OK. *It'll be fine.*

"Plant Patrol has a nice ring to it, actually. Thanks for the suggestion. Davin and I have been doing research into biomes, greenhouses, and indoor farming. We're proposing a total revamp of the school garden, but the only problem is finding the money to make it happen. I've been brainstorming ideas, though. A few local businesses might chip in, but only if we put promotional signs up that say stuff like 'These radishes are sponsored by Megamarket.' We'll see. Oh! I picked up a box of flyers today to put all over school. My slogan is 'Pearl has a plan!' Catchy, right? Do you think I should dip into my savings and hire a skywriter, or would that be too much?"

Rube rolled his eyes and chuckled. "'Pearl has a plan'? Sounds kind of lame. No offense. Who pays attention to that stuff, anyway?"

"The good ones. The ones that *care.* Running for student government is important. Our school is falling apart. We all need to band together and do something about it."

"You really think you're going to change things? Give me a break. You're thirteen years old. No one listens to kids."

"Then we'll *make* them listen. If adults keep failing us, what other choice do we have? You should be helping me, you know. But instead you're here, by yourself, being a sad boy. Which doesn't do anyone any good." Suddenly, Pearl's expression changed as she quickly patted down all of her pockets. "I left the gift card on my dresser! Ugh, that's so annoying." She grumbled while considering an alternate plan. "Hmmmm. My older brother is working at the Sammich Shoppe tonight. Remember when we used to go there together? They'd cover the tables with paper and give us a cup of some janky old crayons. One time, you drew this crazy contraption, like a futuristic amusement park spaceship thingy. I've still got it somewhere."

She kept it. "You . . . kept it?"

"You gave it to me. Of course I kept it. And now that you're becoming Mr. Machine, who knows? Might be worth something one day. Anyway, my brother would probably give us a free plate of fries or something. Wanna go?"

CRASH! Trouble on the second floor. Rube and Pearl raced upstairs and found Bertha cheerfully chewing on one of Rube's machines.

"*Ugh,*" he groaned. "*Why do you do this?!*"

Pearl knelt down to assess the damage and sneak a quick pet. "I've never actually seen any of these machines you've been making. Very interesting. What was this one called?"

"The Fang Polisher. It brushes your teeth. Zach and I were working on it."

"*Groundbreaking*. Or weird and pointless? We'll find out soon enough." Pearl's words were like a knife in Rube's heart. She stabbed him quick, twisted the thing a few times, pulled it out, and then plunged it back in for good measure. *These are my dreams.* Rube's body sank. That's when Pearl knew she'd made a mistake. Her words were meant as a lighthearted joke, but Rube didn't hear them as a playful poke from a friend. She'd never seen him in such a sensitive place. *There's a first time for everything.* "That wasn't fair of me. You're really passionate about making stuff. I can see that. But you haven't shared this side of yourself before. I don't know Rube Goldberg, Machine Maker. Show me."

Rube bristled. *Just show her. What's the problem?* "I don't know."

"Why not? This is what you love, right?" Pearl asked. "Look, I have a passion for baking. If you wanted to watch me make a red velvet cake with cream cheese frosting so you could learn about baking, I'd make it happen." She looked over the remnants of the Fang Polisher with a curious glint in her eye. "How does it work? Put it back together. Take me through the steps. I want to see what you see. Show off that talent."

This feels like a trap. "This feels like a trap."

Pearl laughed. "Man, you're really something else, Goldberg. Fine, don't show me. I'll just go home . . ."

"Wait." Rube sat down on the ground and began putting the machine back together, piece by piece. As he did so, he explained to Pearl how each part worked with the next. "I know this must be boring . . ."

"I'm not bored. It's cool." She'd never seen him take such care and consideration. This wasn't just a hobby. This was Rube's passion. "Can we test it now?" Pearl looked over at Bertha, who was sitting peacefully in the corner. "Want to test the Fang Polisher, girl?"

Why did you just do that?!

Roused by Pearl's request, Bertha twirled across the room like a looney toon, wrecking Rube's creation. Only after watching the color drain from his face did she realize that what she had done was bad. *This is pointless.* Rube fell back his bed and put his head in his hands.

"It's only a temporary defeat." Pearl sat down and put her hand on his shoulder. "Everything can be fixed."

You don't understand. Rube sat up and wiped his nose. "I want to be alone right now."

"I feel you," Pearl said. "But there's something else I need to talk to you about."

Rube launched himself off the bed and dashed downstairs.

"Okay . . ." Pearl looked at Bertha, who wasn't sure what to make of Rube's behavior. They followed him down the stairs together. "I'll get out of your hair in a minute, but we need to talk about Boob."

"Why? Does he need help removing the curse of Gladys the ghost girl?" Rube said with a snarky snicker.

"That's not funny," replied Pearl. "This curse thing is no joke.

Two teachers found mysterious red splatter marks in their classrooms, and Principal Kim is trying to cover it up. I overheard him telling them not to say anything to anyone about it. Just because there's no scientific explanation for paranormal activity, that doesn't mean it's not real. It means we just can't prove it yet. Hopefully, nothing crazy will happen at Con-Con."

Rube gulped. *Hopefully?!*

"And as for Boob, he really needs *you* right now." Rube's ears perked up, and his expression turned serious. "Things have been rough for him lately. Rougher than usual. Mike and Ike have been giving him a hard time when no one else is around. Cornering him after school, following him home, harassing him any chance they can get. It's gotten bad."

"No way. Those guys are total dopes, but I haven't seen them doing *that* kind of stuff. Boob would have told me."

"Just because you don't see something doesn't mean it's not happening."

Suddenly, Rube remembered the curious bruise on Boob's arm. "Then why did he come to *you* and not me? It doesn't make any sense. Boob *promised* to tell me if people were pushing him around."

"He tried to tell you. But you were too busy hanging out with Zach."

Rube didn't like hearing that one bit. It made him angry both at Pearl and at himself. *How did I fail my best friend?* But he already knew the answer. He simply didn't want to admit it. *This isn't the time. I have too much on my plate right now.* Rube's heart started beating so fast, he patted his chest to calm it down. "Don't start with me again!"

"I'm . . . not. Are you okay? It looks like you're having a panic attack . . ."

"Look, I'm sorry you caught feelings, but don't bring *my* best friend into *your* drama." *Oops. I don't think I meant that?* Rube had accidentally gone into attack mode. His words slipped out way harsher than they had when they were swimming around in his head. What's worse was that Rube knew they were a hollow shield. *He* was the one with feelings. He was the one with drama. He'd gotten so worked up that his brain told him to turn the tables on Pearl. His brain was often *very* wrong.

"*Feelings.* Huh. If you say so," Pearl said, folding her arms. She saw right through him. "But the only person here with drama is *you*. If you hadn't pushed away your friends, this wouldn't be happening."

"*You don't understand,*" Rube insisted. "Just leave. Go work on your campaign."

Pearl nodded solemnly. "If that's what you want. But before I

go, you need to know something. Volunteering over the summer made me realize the kind of person that I want to be. I'm ready to use my gifts, share what I have, and give back to this community. So how about this? I'll do *me*. You do *you*."

"Fine."

"Learn a lesson for once, Goldberg," Pearl said.

Rube closed the door and lay down on the couch with Bertha cozy beside him. *I really messed up.* He grabbed his phone and called Boob. No answer. He texted "u there?" No response. Then he noticed a bug crawling around in the light fixture on the ceiling. *Maybe I could make a machine that . . . no, never mind, not now . . .* He called Zach to see if he was coming over. No answer. Then a text popped through. "Can't hang 2 nite." *Welp, that answered that. What to do? What to do?* Rube catapulted himself off the couch, scaring Bertha half to death, and ran up to the attic. He fished his mom's old telescope out of a box and pointed its sight on the Haunted Hideaway. *What are you looking for, exactly? The Professor doesn't want you near him. Mystery solved. Let it go.* But Rube couldn't help himself. He was fascinated by the Professor's existence and wanted to know more about him. After a few minutes of investigation, he spotted a quick flicker in an upstairs bedroom. But upon further inspection, it turned out to be a beam of scattered moonlight breaking through the waving tree limbs.

This is dumb. Rube gave up and went back down to his perch on the couch, where Bertha nuzzled her snout under Rube's chin and licked his face. *Man, her breath stinks like dog butt.*

CHAPTER 9

Whoa . . .

It was the night before Con-Con and all through the school, kids had been building, using their tools. Their machines were now working, *mostly*, to be fair, with the hope they'd win prizes and desirous stares. Students were lurking, some filled with dread, while teachers looked over their shoulders and heads.

But not Rube Goldberg.

Nerves, schmerves. His adrenaline was pumping. He was excited to be in the home stretch. The big show was closer than ever. It finally felt good to share his work with the world. Deciding on his show machine was a grueling process. He poured a lot of blood, sweat, and tears into his babies. Some of them were less than perfect, but they were also pieces of him. Choosing a favorite was hard, especially with so many options at his disposal. When he woke up that morning, it came to him. *The Wakey Wakey Baby.* An alarm clock for a new age. It felt the most Rube-y of all of his recent

creations. A classic in the making. He loved the way it looked when it was in motion, and he couldn't wait to unveil it to the world.

After setting up, Rube strolled through the gym looking at everyone else's contraptions. It was like a garden of invention. Each machine produced its own strange fruit. Groups were arranging their booths, straightening their signs, and putting the finishing touches on their masterpieces. *There's some fierce competition out here.* But none of it truly scared him. Charlie Stoffregen and Karl Jones created a device called the Couch Potato that held a bag of potato chips and a drink while you played video games. *A fun concept, but not a contraption.* Jaida and Heidi Hall made a gadget called the Beautifier that puts makeup on your face while you're sleeping. *Scary.* One group of seventh graders, the Lords of B-Town, created the Personal Pic-Taker, which was really just a reclining chair outfitted with a selfie stick. *Unoriginal.* When it came to other people's work, Rube could spot flaws and missteps a mile away. He remembered them vividly and always filed them away in his head for future reference. That way *he'd* never make the mistakes other people made. Or so he thought.

"Will our machines be safe here overnight?" Charlie asked.

"Absolutely," replied Principal Kim. "We've hired extra security."

"You'll beat 'em all and reign supreme!" Boob's words poked Rube in the back of his head, then tap-danced their way through his brain till they were front and center. He couldn't stop thinking about them. *Is being number one really all that important?* The *making* was the thing that kept him going. The *doing* inspired him to work harder. How would any of that change if he lost? *It's not like losing will stop me from doing what I love.* The revelation washed over him, and suddenly, *winning* didn't seem to hold the same weight. It was cool, of course, and who doesn't want to win prizes? But winning didn't mean something was the absolute best. *Sometimes it did.* But not always.

As Rube strolled past the rest of the contraptions, the burden that he'd been carrying seemed to lessen. A new perspective began to form. *As long as I keep my head down and focus on doing the best I can, I don't need to worry about competition.*

And then he turned a corner.

What Rube saw next was so unexpected and so infuriating that his temper ignited immediately.

Zach was in his booth, assembling a machine that helped you put a shirt on. He called it *The Jiggler.*

"What the fuzz do you think you're doing!?" Rube growled. "That's *my* design."

"Whoa, whoa, whoa," Zach said. "Relax, tough guy."

Rube whipped out his notebook and showed him the page. "*You stole my machine.*" There was no denying it. Zach's Jiggler looked exactly like Rube's. Except better. "All those times you flipped through my notebook . . . you planned this . . ."

"Man, all I did was borrow the name. I've been building *my* machine for a long while now. I wasn't going to enter it into the contest because I knew you had one like it already. But then you went with something else, so I figured I'd give it a shot. You really think I need to *steal* from you?"

"Liar-y liar!" Boob exclaimed. He'd been waiting nearby to say hello to Rube. "Those swoopy black bangs don't fool me, cheese stealer. You've been up to something from the start, and now we

 all know what it was—"

"Calm down, String Bean," Zach said. "This is none of your business."

Boob looked at Rube. "Are you going to let this guy talk to me like that?"

"Crawl back to your trailer park," Zach taunted. "The smart people are talking."

Rube's nerves frayed. He was frozen in place.

What is happening here?! There were too many things happening at once. He didn't know how to process any of it. He couldn't think straight. The situation made him deeply uncomfortable and embarrassed. But instead of taking action, he closed up and stayed silent.

"So . . . nothing?" Boob asked. He fished around in his pocket and pulled out a purple crystal attached to a silver chain. It was just like the one he'd bought on vacation. "Special-ordered this specter protector from a guy in New Mexico." He tossed it at Rube, hitting him on the cheek. "My mom helped me track it down. Used up all my allowance. Rushed delivery so you'd have it for tomorrow. Good luck." Boob stormed out of the gym in anger.

"He got you a . . . crystal . . . that protects you from . . . specters?" Zach asked. "That kid is obsessed with you."

"That *kid* has been my best friend for as long as I've been alive. Don't you *ever* talk about him again," Rube growled. He knelt down and picked up the crystal pendant.

"Look, I didn't mean to cause any trouble—"

"Shut up!" Rube barked.

Mr. Blank noticed a commotion brewing. He raced over to handle the matter before it got out of control. "I don't know what's going on here, but I suggest you lower your voices. Come with me, Rueben." He walked over to Rube's display, where the Wakey Wakey Baby was covered with a tarp. "You seem to be ahead of

the game, from what I can see," he said, peeking underneath. "There will be plenty of time tomorrow morning, before the competition begins, to perform trials and do any last-minute tinkering. Go home. Clear your mind. Get some rest."

"But—"

"You've come this far." Mr. Blank put his hand on Rube's shoulder. "Don't let anger and frustration get the best of you. *Use* it."

Rube nodded in agreement. He was thrown by the incident and confused as to what to do next. But Mr. Blank made sense. *Keep your head down and do what he says. The guy knows what he's talking about.* On his way out, Rube noticed Mike and Ike lingering in a corner, scrolling through their phones privately. Neither of them had a machine to show. *It doesn't make sense.*

On the way home, Rube rode past all of his favorite places and tried not to think about Con-Con. It wasn't the least bit easy. His machine felt solid, which was a relief. He had worked out all the kinks during the trial phase, and there wasn't much else he could do but relax. Not that the situation with Zach and Boob hadn't upset him. There was simply nothing he could do about it at the moment. *Everything will work out fine. It has to.* As Rube walked in the door, he was greeted by his favorite smell (and Bertha). Grandma Etta had left him a big plate of chicken dumplings, which he promptly scarfed down. After that, it was all about zoning out on the couch and watching cartoons. It was the first time he'd done that in a good long while. It felt nice. A few hours later, after a series of prolonged yawns, it was officially time to hit the hay. Rube trudged upstairs, brushed his teeth, and tried his best to go to sleep, but it was hard for him to seal the deal. His body was tired, but his mind raced. *Right before bed. Typical.*

He worried about Boob, wished he'd listened to Pearl, and felt betrayed by Zach. But most of all, Rube missed his mom. *No offense, Dad.* She often crept into his thoughts late at night. He'd remember her smile and the gentle way she'd brush the hair out of his eyes whenever he'd get upset. Sometimes it was comforting. Tonight, it was painful. He wanted to wrap his arms around her and ask for advice. She was good at that kind of thing, never pushing, always guiding. Her hugs were tight in the best possible way. Not having her around left a humongous hole in Rube's heart. He'd been trying to fill it, but the darn thing just didn't want to heal.

The later it got, the more he tossed and turned. He'd drift off to sleep and wake up unexpectedly. Then, suddenly, it was morning.

There's no going back now.

He arrived at school and found hordes of students waiting to be let into the gym. It seemed like everyone had some last-minute Con-Con preparations to take care of. Rube spotted Boob from across the hallway, but they pretended not to see each other. At the moment, there wasn't anything Rube could have said or done that would've fixed the situation. *Better to just keep on walking, and talk when everything is over.*

"Excuse me," Principal Kim said, pushing through the mob. "I know it's a big day and we're all excited, but I need you all to *move.*" The crowd parted amicably, and he unlocked the doors. "Thank you." As students rushed by him, feverishly flooding into the space, their excitement quickly turned to shock. Displays had been overturned and banners ripped down. The gym looked like a tank had rolled through it. Every single machine had been destroyed.

"What the . . . ?"

Pandemonium broke loose. Some kids cried out in anger, others in shock. Ike took video of the whole thing, laughing as he noticed bits of neon orange slime bestrewed throughout the space. "The ghost strikes again!" he shouted, elbowing his brother in the rib.

Rube quietly uncovered the Wakey Wakey Baby and found it

torn to shreds. Each piece had been individually broken so it couldn't be put back together. In shock, he quietly sat down on the ground, surrounded by destruction. Then he looked over at Zach's display. *You've got to be kidding me.* There wasn't a hair out of place. It was the only machine that hadn't been touched. Rube's heart began beating out of his chest.

He'd never had a full-on anxiety attack before, but it sure felt like he was having one now. His mouth couldn't form words. He hyperventilated, his body quaking with emotion. *I'vegottogetoutofhere.*

While everyone was preoccupied, Rube walked out the door, hopped on his bike, and rushed home. There was no way he was staying at school for the rest of the day.

He was done.

With everything.

No more making. No more building. *No more machines.*

He walked in the door, raced upstairs, and got into bed. Dark thoughts crept into his head as he pulled the covers over his face and sobbed.

It's all your fault. Why even try if all you're going to do is fail? Just give up.

No. What happened was out of my control. I did the best I could. Keep going.

I did the best I could.

Keep going.

I did the best I could.

Keep going.

Bertha snuggled next to him as he fell asleep fully clothed.

When he finally woke up, it was nighttime. *Whoa. I must've really needed the rest.* Low thunderclaps rolled in the distance as the warm autumn rain pitter-pattered on the roof. Dazed and groggy, Rube ventured through the pitch-black house to the kitchen, where he downed a glass of orange juice. There were missed calls and voice mails he didn't care to check. He called his dad a couple times, but it went straight to voice mail. *Must be doing business-y business.*

Before going to her Bridge Club, Grandma dropped off a bowl of macaroni salad and a giant spoon. Rube dug into it like a ravenous beast as he watched the rain fall, out the window. Then, in the distance, he noticed a light turn on in the attic of the Haunted Hideaway. *DON'T EVEN THINK ABOUT IT. The Professor warned you not to come back. The guy has lasers, remember?!* But Rube desperately needed to talk to someone who understood the way his brain worked. The Professor was the only person around at the moment who fit that bill. "Bertha, guard the house. I'll be back in a little bit." He ditched his macaroni salad and marched down the street in the drizzle. The gate was locked, so he jimmied it open and trudged up the hill once again. Rube noticed a plethora of new additions to the majestic sea of junk outside the Professor's home. *Looks like someone is cleaning house. I wonder what that's all about.* He forced himself not to browse, though he still longed for that accordion rack. *But now is not the time.* Instead of ringing the doorbell like a normal person, Rube went with a more outspoken approach.

"PROFESSOR!" he yelled at the top of his lungs.

Minutes passed with no response, though the light in the window remained. *He's ignoring me.* The rainfall quickened, and the wind picked up. *There's no point.* Rube quietly sat down on the ground cross-legged and put his head in his hands. The weight of the past month hit at him, all at once. *I did this to myself.* In that moment, he felt defeated and alone. *What am I even doing here? I'm such a failure.* Then the front door swung open. *FWOOSH!*

"Stop being dramatic

and get in here!" the Professor shouted. "The last thing I need is a sullen, weepy child on my lawn. I've already got enough problems with this town as it is." He waved Rube into the house and closed the door behind them. "I *knew* I should have installed a shark-filled moat around this property when I had the chance."

"Sorry," Rube sniffled. He was in a daze. The Professor motioned to follow him down the hallway, and as they walked, Rube spotted something he hadn't noticed the first time around. A large steel door had mysteriously appeared. It was shiny silver and covered in padlocks. "What's in *there*?" he asked.

"A giant hybrid cyborg monster I made using the DNA of all neighborhood children," the Professor replied. "Mind your own business."

The duo entered the living room, which had been tidied up and thoroughly dusted since Rube's last visit. "You finally cleaned the place," Rube said. "Looks good."

The Professor groaned. "Oh, to be complimented by a child. What a wondrous feeling. Nice night to have an emotional breakdown on a stranger's property, eh?"

"You're not a stranger to me. Not anymore."

"I let you into my house *one time* and all of a sudden you think we know each other. Tsk, tsk, tsk. See, *this* is why I don't mentor. I have a bad habit of attracting strays."

"*I'm not a stray*," Rube fumed.

"My apologies. That came out incorrectly. I've been on edge ever since this town served me with papers. Told me I have one week to clean up my yard or they'll sue me. One week! As if I'm made of time." The Professor sighed. "So, what seems to be the problem *this* evening? Need a hand fixing a broken phone? Trouble with your algebra homework? Or are you simply obsessed with me like everyone else?"

"I just needed to talk to someone."

"Ugh. This again? *Call your friends!*"

"*I can't! They're all mad at me!*"

The Professor smirked. "Ahhh. At last the truth comes out." He went to the kitchen and poured two cups of tea. "Drink this," he said, handing one to Rube. "It'll calm you. I swear it's not poison." The Professor ambled over to an old reclining chair, plopped himself down, and relaxed. "What happened? Give me the bullet points."

Rube took a sip of tea. "Middle school is a joke."

"That machine-building competition was a bust, eh?"

"Pretty much. Someone destroyed *my* machine and everyone else's."

"Oof! Well, *that* sounds dreadful. Human beings can be so dis-

appointing. Assuming humans were behind it. One never knows around here."

"What's *that* supposed to mean?"

"Look, Rube, things fall apart all the time." The Professor shrugged. "Sometimes it's our fault. Sometimes it's the fault of others. But things also get rebuilt, so I wouldn't worry about it. You'll recover."

"You're terrible at giving advice."

"Who said that was advice?!" the Professor snapped. "It's *reality*."

"You don't understand."

"Oh please. I understand more about you than you understand about yourself. I'm ancient! And wise. Trust me. My underwear is older than you."

"Ewww." Rube noticed a disassembled machine on the Professor's kitchen table. He picked up its parts, inspecting each one. "What are you working on?"

"Hands off! Back to the matter at hand." The Professor launched himself out of his chair and began pacing around the room. "When I was a younger person, I thought I could do everything on my own. I didn't want help. I didn't want advice. I was stupid. *Stupid, stupid, stupid.* I pushed away the people who meant

the most to me, all because I didn't want to listen to anyone else but myself." He pointed to the newspaper article on the wall. "Remember ol' Professor Zeero? When I was busy pushing everyone away, he swooped in and took advantage of the situation. He stole my work! I'd say he helped turn my friends against me, but I did a fairly good job of that all by myself. I was blinded by my own ambition. Now I'm the crazy old kook who lives all alone in a haunted house . . ." He trailed off, gazing at his wall of accomplishments. "It's not as fun as the life I once had, that's for sure."

"So, this house *is* haunted. I knew it!"

"*You're not paying attention.*" The Professor scurried back into the kitchen for another cup of tea. "Open your eyes, Rueben.

It's *obvious* you let your machine making consume you, and it's *obvious* you pushed all of your friends away in the process. Don't you see what you're becoming? *Me.*"

Wow. He really went there. Rube did the math in his head, and everything checked out exactly as the Professor described. It took hearing someone else say the words for him to see the unvarnished truth. "But you're a world-renowned inventor," Rube said. "There are worse things to be, I guess."

"I've got a family of raccoons in the attic that I feed twice a week, my toenails are as long as licorice strands, and technically I haven't bathed in a month," the Professor said with a sly smile. "If you want to keep on doing things *your* way, go right ahead."

"No, thanks." Rube winced. "But what am I supposed to do?"

"I'm not giving you *all* the answers. Think about it."

The first answer is obvious. "I should apologize to my friends."

"And yourself," the Professor said, sipping his tea. "I know you've probably been beating yourself up inside that gigantic head of yours. And I can tell you from experience, it's not healthy. It's cruel and unfair. So *cut it out*. Say you're sorry." He pointed to Rube's reflection in the mirror.

"Um, no. That's weird." Rube looked at himself, turning his head in every direction and eyeing each and every little detail. "What's going on with my hair these days? It's really out of control."

"*This is not about looks*," the Professor growled. "Fine, then. How about this instead? Whenever you're feeling down about the state of things, do something nice for someone."

"Hahahahaha," Rube chuckled. The Professor wasn't laughing. "Oh. You're serious."

"You came here for wisdom, boy. *Soak. It. Up.*"

"Okay." Rube thought about the Professor's proposal for a moment. "That's *extra*, but I guess I see the value. If I do something nice for someone, it'll make me feel better."

"No, you do something nice for someone because it makes *them* feel better. Do it because they need you to set a good example. Do it because people need care and support. Not because it gives you a jolly little feeling. Which it might. But that's beside the point."

"Weird advice coming from a guy who never leaves his house. What nice things have *you* done for someone else lately?"

"*Look in the mirror and find out.*" The Professor glanced at the clock. "It's been a real treat trying to break your stubborn little shell, but I need you to leave."

"Are your TV shows about to start?"

"No. I just don't want you here any longer," the Professor said. He beckoned Rube to follow, and as they walked down the hallway, the faint cries of an animal were heard deep inside the bowels of the Haunted Hideaway. *It's probably nothing.* The Professor opened the drapes a smidge and peered out the window. "The rain stopped, so you won't melt. Once you get home, play some of your favorite music. And all your problems will simply drift away."

"Cool."

"I was joking! But in all honesty, music helps." The Professor sighed. "All of this stress, all of this toiling. And for what?! Mankind's capacity for exerting maximum effort with minimal results never fails to astound." As he opened the front door, the brisk smell of rain wafted into the house. It was a refreshing change of pace. "Rube, for as long as I can remember, you're the only person who had the apples to knock on my door and stay there until I opened it. You're a *bold* kid. I like that about you. Even though you smell."

That's it!

"*Be bold*," Rube muttered to himself. "The answer was staring me in the face the whole dang time." A flood of new ideas began stewing inside his brain. He raced down the steps into the trash garden. "Please please please tell me I can have that accordion rack."

"Take whatever you want. Then leave and *don't come back*," the Professor said, slamming the door. He shouted from inside the house. "I mean it this time!"

It's going to be a long night.

CHAPTER 10

The students of Beechwood Middle School had been anxiously sitting in the auditorium for the past twenty minutes. With the air-conditioning broken, the room was quickly growing hotter. Assemblies had become a common occurrence lately, but this one was slightly different. Principal Kim was about to make a big announcement about Con-Con *and* the ghost. Rumors spread around school that police cars were spotted out front, waiting to take kids away to jail. Rube was nowhere to be found. He hadn't shown up for class. He hadn't answered any messages. Boob and Pearl weren't just worried, they were scared.

"Still nothing?" asked Pearl.

Boob shook his head. "Do you think he ran away and is living down by the train tracks near the dump? I bet he's fishing in the river with his bare hands."

"That kid can't catch a fish with a fishing pole. He sure as heck can't catch one with his hands. What if—" she said, stopping short. "No. That's too crazy."

"*What's* too crazy?!" Boob exclaimed. "You can't say *that's too crazy*, then abandon ship. Spill it, girl!"

Pearl hesitated. "What if Rube was the ghost all along?"

"You were right the first time," Boob replied. "That's *too* crazy."

"Think about it, though. He was so worried about Con-Con. Maybe the ghost was one big distraction to help take the pressure off himself in case he didn't deliver the goods. People self-sabotage all the time. Sometimes they don't even know they're doing it."

"Back it up, Nancy Drew. Just because Rube ghosted *us* doesn't mean—" Boob gasped. "Oh no. You're right. He's the ghost. Rube is the ghost! Maybe not. But maybe yes! Is it hot in here, or am I losing my mind?"

Zach sat down behind them. "Have either of you talked to Rube?"

Boob swung around, putting his finger in Zach's face. "No, we haven't, you treacherous snake," he snapped. "You machine-stealing piece of—"

"*Relax*, Boob," Pearl said. "He's not worth it."

"I didn't do anything wrong," replied Zach. "How do we know *you're* not the one behind all this junk? You just *happened* to find a creepy doll in the woods that unleased a curse upon the school? Yeah, right. *You wanted attention*. Rube and I became buddies, and you got all butt-hurt about it. You've been jealous from the very beginning. Who else would know exactly how to hurt him but his best friend in the world?"

Boob boiled with anger. "If it was *me*, I would have beat your machine to shreds too, you oozing-pus goblin." Pearl put her hand on his shoulder to calm him down.

"I'll take it from here," she said. "Hi, Zach. We haven't officially met. I'm Pearl. Also, Rube's friend. I think it might be best if you keep your thoughts to yourself on this one. Okay?"

"You're probably in on it too," Zach replied. "I'm sure it would help your campaign if everything fell apart so only *you* could put it back together."

"Excuse me!?" Pearl exclaimed. "First of all, that's insane. Second of all, you don't know what you're talking about. And! Your breath smells like rotten eggs."

Principal Kim hurried into the auditorium. It was clear from the dark circles under his eyes that he'd had a very long night. The room quieted immediately as he prepared to speak. "Here at Beechwood Middle School, we are a family. Through thick and thin. No matter what. I know we're all confused and heartbroken over what happened to Con-Con. The local police have informed me that because our security cameras are, in their words, 'in desperate need of an upgrade,' we've been unable to use the footage to help find the person or *persons* responsible for these despicable acts. If you or anyone you know has any information, I urge you to come forward and share it so we can catch the culprit."

"Ask Gladys the Ghost!" a voice called out.

"Yes, Gladys. *The ghost.* I will be addressing *that* shortly." His hand trembled as he took a sip of bottled water. "In the meantime, I'd like to say . . ." He glanced over at Mr. Blank, who nodded solemnly. "Unfortunately, due to timing and a host of other financial difficulties, we won't be able to remount Con-Con this year. That also means the winner of the competition, by default, *because his was the only contraption left standing*, is Zachary Billingsley."

A wave of whispers quickly moved through the crowded room. "This is bull honky!" Boob shouted. "We demand a do-over!"

Suddenly, the auditorium door swung open, causing everyone to turn. Lala Palooza had a bullhorn, and she was not afraid to use it. "Tout le monde dehors! Nous allons faire une excursion sur le terrain. Quelqu'un a-t-il déjà conduit une limousine? J'en ai quarante prêtes et en attente." Then she realized she was speaking French. "Sorry about that. Everyone outside! We're taking a field trip," she explained. "Ever ride in a limo? I've got forty of them ready and waiting."

"*Excuse me*, Miss Palooza. You can't just barge in here and kidnap the entire student body," said Principal Kim. "We will *not* be a part of some kind of flash mob."

Lala winced. "Flash mob? Ugh. No one does that anymore, Grandpa. Trust me. This is really important. And it'll be quick. Promise. You wanted attention, right, Principal Kim?"

"What?!" exclaimed Principal Kim. "I . . . don't . . . this . . . is . . ." He stumbled to find a way out of admitting the truth. "Who said that?"

"*Everyone*. Now buckle up, because you're about to get more attention than you can handle."

Students launched out of their seats and raced outside to find a line of limos that stretched around the block. It was a breathtaking sight. They piled into them without a second thought. Principal Kim tried to stop everyone, but in the end, all he could do was follow.

"What's this about?" Boob said wearily.

"Just get in and don't ask questions." Pearl pushed him into a limo, and off they went. The fleet of automobiles drove through Beechwood, winding around the streets like a long robot serpent. Eventually, they arrived at a familiar destination—7483 Berkeley Street, Rube's house. There were big screen TVs set up outside, in formation. As students gathered on the lawn, Rube appeared at his bedroom window. "Hey, everyone! Things are a little tight inside. If you were involved in Con-Con, come on in! If you can't fit, hang out here for a bit. You'll all get a chance to see what I've cooked up, just as soon as possible," he said, closing the curtain.

"What about us?" Boob asked Pearl. "We weren't involved in Con-Con."

"He'll make an exception," Pearl replied.

As students crowded themselves inside the house, Rube slid down the banister to greet them. He even dressed up for the occasion. "Thanks for coming!" he said, adjusting the collar of his sleek little suit. "Welcome to my place." He pointed at the living room, which was walled off with a curtain. "But don't go in there. *Yet.* Otherwise, let me give you the tour." Jaws dropped as everyone made their way through the space. Rube had turned his home into a wonderland of machines. His entire house had become a magical museum of invention.

"I demand an explanation!" Principal Kim stormed in, ready to go ballistic. Instead, he was left breathless. "This . . . is . . . *beautiful.* What have you done, Rueben?"

"Wait a minute," said Jaida Hall, inspecting one of the machines. "This is mine and my sister's. This is the *Beautifier.* Did you—"

"Rebuild each and every one of the machines that got destroyed? Yep! I remembered their construction really clearly. To be perfectly honest, I couldn't get a few of them out of my head. Some needed improvements, which I made, while others were more or

less sturdy to begin with. But the idea for each one came from the team who made it, not me. All I really did was set them up. The placard under each one lists the team name and all the members. Obviously, they wouldn't all fit in my house, so make sure you check out the backyard as well. There's a whole bunch back there too."

Principal Kim was in shock. "This is amazing. How . . . did you do all of this?"

"I stayed up all night drinking Beefcake Fuel," Rube replied. "Just kidding. Power naps were key." He opened his mouth as wide as it could go and released a long, loud yawn. "But I could really use a good night's sleep." As students moved through the house, marveling at the inventive assemblage, Rube spotted Pearl and Boob in the corner and gave them a shy, awkward wave. There was so much he wanted to say, but it wasn't the time. Pearl and Boob smiled as they returned the gesture.

Watching Rube move through the room was the best part. He was a superb master of ceremonies. In that moment, Pearl and Boob understood what building machines meant to their best friend. It was clear from Rube's giddy expression that he was in his happy place and finally at ease sharing his gift with the world. It was a huge step. They wanted to give him a big, proud hug. But there were too many people around for that kind of lovefest. For now, Boob and Pearl were content watching Rube enjoy himself.

"It was you!" Zach angrily pushed himself into the room. "*You* sabotaged Con-Con and did all of this just to make yourself look like a hero. And everyone's falling for it!" Bertha growled as Zach got closer to Rube.

"That's not true, Zach. All I wanted to do was make it up to the teams who worked so hard. Their machines deserve to be seen and appreciated. So does yours." He gestured to a replica of Zach's machine. "I'm sorry that I thought you stole my design. Great minds think alike, and it wasn't fair of me to accuse you without proof." Mr. Blank entered in silence, taking in the sight. "You're right on time, Mr. Blank. Please follow me," Rube said, opening the living room curtain to reveal his newest mechanical creation. "I present to you my pièce de résistance! Otherwise known as . . ." He trailed off for a moment. "I'll tell you in a minute. The name is a spoiler. In the meantime, we'll call it the Mystery Machine! Have a seat, Mr. Blank. Best one in the house." Rube patted the cushions of a big, comfy chair in the corner of the room.

"And what is the purpose of this device?" asked Mr. Blank.

Rube grinned. "You'll see." He had everyone's attention. *This is the moment of truth. Here goes . . . something.* He set the machine in motion, each step executing perfectly. Even Bertha got in on the action. Mr. Blank was intrigued by the device, but as it advanced toward its goal, he came to a

realization. He'd been tricked. Before he could do anything about it, a metal claw descended from above. It ripped off his hairpiece, uncovering a shiny bald head with a very familiar splotch-shaped birthmark on his cranium.

What the whaaaaaaat!

Rube's mouth fell open. Students doubled over with laughter, not knowing the truth behind this shocking discovery. Fuming, Mr. Blank sprang from the chair and made a beeline for the door. Luckily, Bertha jumped into action and stopped his escape, growling and barking till he sat down.

"Y-you're him?" Rube stuttered. "But you're supposed to be dead."

Principal Kim wanted answers. "Quiet down, everyone! Quiet down," he said. "Can someone please explain what's going on here?!"

Rube raised his hand "Um, so, this is really weird, but Mr. Blank is actually an international criminal mastermind named Professor Zeero."

"*For real?*" asked Boob. "An international criminal ended up *here*? In Beechwood? We don't even have a Bubba Burger. Plus, the weather is meh."

"I can explain . . ." *Good luck getting anyone to believe you, Goldberg.* "So, there's this, um, world-famous inventor named Professor Butts. He and Zeero, the guy *we* know as Mr. Blank, used to be pals back in the day. But Zeero betrayed the Professor. Then died? To be perfectly honest, I'm super confused right now."

"The report of my death was an exaggeration," Mr. Blank snarled. "It took me years to find your friend, the *Professor*, after he hid himself in this disgusting little town. Once I arrived here, my plan to destroy him took a different shape. I'd hurt *him* by hurting *you*. Any friend of *Butts* is my enemy." The house erupted with laughter. "Oh, when Rube says *Butts*, it's fine, but when *I* say it, you laugh? Nasty, stinking little brats. May you all rot."

"You built me up just so you could tear me down," said Rube. "An agent of chaos. Just like the Professor said. I *knew* Con-Con had to be an inside job."

"I'd like to speak to my lawyer," Mr. Blank replied. "Unless, perhaps, Principal Kim has something he'd like to add?"

"Well . . . I . . . this is really . . . not . . . a good time . . ." Principal Kim sputtered, twisting his body as if he had to use the bathroom.

"Tell them!" Mr. Blank shouted. "If you don't, *I will.*"

"This is getting spicy," whispered Boob. "I'm into it."

"Mr. Blank—I mean, *Professor Zeero*—is the ghost too, right?" Pearl asked. "Or am I missing something?"

"Not *exactly*." Principal Kim collapsed into a nearby chair. "Beechwood Middle School needs money. *Badly*. Our funding was cut by the state. Senator Wharfman said education isn't his top priority, and that has left us in deep, deep trouble. When the ghost rumors started, I thought if the local news was interested, maybe we could go viral and make a few bucks. We could sell T-shirts and give tours of America's First Haunted Middle School. I'm ashamed to admit it, but *I* staged the slime incident. It was so *stupid* of me.

No one got hurt, thank goodness. Mr. Blank found out about what I did and threatened to expose me. I planned on telling everyone the truth, but then everything happened with Con-Con, which I had absolutely *nothing* to do with. And I *certainly* didn't know about any of this Professor Zeero business." He put his head in his hands and sobbed. "I messed up. I did what I thought was right and ended up making a fool of myself. Now the school will never get the resources we need."

"I've got you covered." Lala reached into her purse, retrieved

a slip of paper, and placed it in Principal Kim's hand. "Pearl and I have been talking lately. She's got a lot of good ideas. One of them got me thinking. I might be *stuck* in public school, but there's no reason I can't try to use my family's money to make things a little better around here."

As Principal Kim unfolded the slip of paper, his eyes widened. It was a check for a *large* sum of money. "Lala, this is . . . un . . . believable . . ."

"Just a little donation. No strings attached," Lala said. "But cash it quick, before my parents get home. Just kidding! That amount of money is literally nothing to them. Oh, and start a STEM program too, while you're at it. As a treat."

Suddenly, Officer Bacon barged into the house, blaring his bullhorn. "WHOEVER OWNS THOSE LIMOS OUTSIDE NEEDS TO MOVE THEM ASAP OR FACE SWIFT JUSTICE! And, uh, I think I'm here to arrest someone."

"*That guy*," Boob said, pointing to Mr. Blank. "Don't worry, Mr. Zeero. Officer Bacon is a superb driver. Not the best conversationalist. But one out of two ain't bad, right?"

"Okay, everybody back in the limos!" Lala shouted. "My parents will freak out if they knew I took them." She paused, bursting into a big smile. "Just kidding! I can do anything I want."

"Thanks for helping me put all of this together, Lala," Rube said. "I owe you one."

"I know, Goldberg," Lala replied. "And one day *very* soon, I'll come to collect."

Officer Bacon put Mr. Blank in handcuffs and walked him out of the house, onto the front lawn, for the entire neighborhood to see. It was the most interesting thing to happen to Beechwood in quite a while.

"Bye!" Rube said, waving. "Thanks for living up to *both* of your names!"

Mr. Blank glared. "I'm humbled by this embarrassment. That

much is true. But this isn't the end, dear boy. Not by a long shot. You see, I play a *very* long game."

Rube held his hand up to his ear. "Did you say *lawn* game?"

"A *long* game."

"A lawn game? Like . . . a game you play on your lawn?"

"No!" shouted Mr. Blank. "A *long* game! A game that is *long*!"

Rube chuckled. "I heard you the first time, idiot."

Rube watched with pleasure as Mr. Blank was put into the police car and driven away to jail. *Or wherever they take bad guys these days.* He never expected in a million years that he'd end up unintentionally unmasking an international criminal. All he wanted to do was make people laugh. Soon a reporter from a local TV station snuck into the house with a camera crew in tow. *Uh-oh. Here we go.* She rushed over to Rube and shoved a microphone in his face. "Hi, I'm Candace Honeywell with BTV News. You're the first child in the tristate area to unmask an alleged criminal mastermind. How does that *feel?*"

Rube cleared his throat and leaned into the mic. "Eh. He was heavy on the criminal but light on the mastermind. And I'm not a child. Allow me to show you around."

The reporter stepped through the house carefully, taking in the majesty of what Rube had built. "This looks like so much fun. What do you call this one?" she asked, pointing at the machine that revealed Professor Zeero.

"Well, it was originally the Wig Flipper, but now it feels more like a—"

Boob snatched the mic and took charge. "It's called a *Rube Goldberg Machine*. One of a kind in every way. Look for us on social media. #RubeGoldbergMachine. That'll be all. Boob out!" he shouted, tossing the microphone away. Rube smiled.

A Rube Goldberg Machine. Yeah, let's go with that.

EPILOGUE

After weeks of drama, Rube was finally able to achieve something he never thought was possible—a full night's rest. No tossing. No turning. No waking up at 4:00 A.M. thinking about global warming. When he rose from his bed the following day, he felt refreshed and renewed. Even had time to sketch a new machine before breakfast. Fixed the air-conditioning too, albeit a little too late. He wanted to stop by the Professor's house and tell him everything that had gone down, but ultimately he decided against it. *The guy doesn't want to be bothered. And besides, the Professor watches so much TV, he probably heard about Zeero's takedown already.* Rube still had a million questions and wondered if he'd ever get the chance to ask them. When he arrived at school, Rube was no longer a nameless kid in the crowd. He was *Rube Goldberg*, the machine kid, sixth-grade hero, unmasker of villainy. It was a lot to process. Everyone wanted their photograph taken with him, but Principal Kim kept swooping in to remind them of the NO PHONES policy. Rube had the entire school's attention, whether he wanted it or not. People complimented him and told him they were inspired by what he did. But more attention meant more pressure. All of a sudden, he had

a target on his back. He wasn't stressed about it. *Yet.* Rube was so wrapped up in giving statements, doing interviews, and, believe it or not, studying, that he hadn't seen his friends.

BRRRRRRRRRING!

When the final bell rang, it was time to make amends. As Rube walked outside, his stomach twisted itself into knots. His nerves flared up again with a vengeance. The thought of facing his friends made him both happy and anxious. They deserved more than a simple apology.

A girl brushed by Rube, knocking into his shoulder. "Oh. Em. Gee." It was Emilia Harris, one of the most popular sixth graders

in the tristate area. Her mom was famous for owning a chain of goat yoga studios. "Those things at your house were so weird. But also cool. Sometimes weird is cool. It's *so* weird."

"Your machine sucked, Goldberg!" Mike shouted.

"Thank you," Rube said with a dramatic bow. "So does yours. Oh wait! You didn't make one, because you lack brainpower *and* creativity. Now, get out of my way. I have an announcement to make." He climbed up the nearest tree, as high as his legs would take him, and perched himself on a sturdy branch. "Can I have your attention, please?" Everyone stopped moving. All eyes were on Rube. "My friend Pearl is running for sixth-grade class president. She's got lots of cool ideas like, um, adding a taco buffet to the lunchroom and building an indoor water park." Pearl was slightly embarrassed by Rube's unexpected proclamation.

"None of that is true," she said under her breath.

"In conclusion, a vote for Pearl is a vote for . . . wha . . . whoa—" Rube's foot slipped on a piece of loose bark, causing him to lose his footing and fall to the ground with a *THUD*. "I'm okay! Don't worry. Just bruised the ol' behind."

"You think you're something special now, don't you, little Rubey?" Ike hovered over Rube, shoving a phone in his face and spitting as he talked. "But nobody cares about you or your dumb machines." Before Ike could continue his thought, Rube flailed his legs uncontrollably, like they'd come alive with electricity. He kicked Ike in the groin, causing him to double over in pain and fall to his knees. "Muh . . . muh . . . muh . . ."

"Oh man, I'm so sorry," said Rube. "My legs have these crazy spasms sometimes. Should I see a doctor? I should probably see a doctor, right?" He leaned in close to Ike's face. "If you ever lay a hand on Boob again, I can promise you it won't just be my foot that has an unexpected outburst. You know what I mean?" Ike mouthed the word "yes." He was in too much pain to speak. Rube took the phone from his hand and tossed it into the field nearby. "Go fetch."

"This isn't over, Goldberg," Mike said, helping Ike to his feet. "Watch your back, 'cause you just made a new enemy."

"You guys are *killing me* with these tired old lines," Rube said, rolling his eyes. "Oh no. A new enemy! I'm very, very scared now. Get in line, Bigfoot." As Mike and Ike shuffled away along with the rest of the crowd, though, a couple of familiar faces came forward to say hello.

"*Ballsy* move, Goldberg," said Pearl.

"Yeah, that was *nuts*," Boob said.

"Ahhh. *My people.* I missed you two," Rube said. "But shut up right now. I really need to say something." He took a long, deep breath. "I've been a complete donkey dimple these past few weeks."

"You used my alternative curse words! All is forgiven."

"Not so fast," Pearl warned. "Rube, continue."

"It's like this . . ." He bit his lip, thinking of the right way to say what was on his mind. "Sometimes I *feel* alone, so then I *think* I'm alone, even though I'm *not* alone. And I guess that makes me push people away. It's like my brain works against me sometimes. Con-Con took over my life, and I didn't see things the way they really were. Bottom line—I shouldn't have tried to do everything by myself. I was *supremely* rude, and I'm really sorry I hurt you both."

"Apology accepted. We didn't know how much you loved making machines. Now we do. But you should still do a weird dance in front of the whole school as punishment for your crimes against friendship," Boob said with a sly grin. "I volunteer myself as choreographer."

"What *he* said, but without the weird dancing," said Pearl. "I'm sure your dad was super excited when you told him you won Con-Con."

Uh-oh. He hadn't spoken to his father in days. Max was still on the road, and Rube didn't want to bother him. "He was happy for me . . ." *Gah! Don't say that, dummy. Just tell the truth.* "Um, actually, that's not true. I haven't called my dad. He's been really busy. But I'll tell him soon."

Pearl put her hand on Rube's shoulder. "Don't wait too long."

223

"When were you going to tell us you know a guy named Professor *Butts*?! That's totally weird and crazy," Boob said. "Do you think he'd want to go into business with me? We could be *Boob & Butts: Attorneys-at-Law*! I'd do funny local commercials and make personal appearances at my uncle's used-car dealership. Our catchphrase could be 'When the odds are *stacked*, we'll get to the *bottom* of things!' I'll even give you a cut of our profits."

"Yeah, about that . . ." *They don't need to know about Professor Butts. It's too much to explain. Besides, the guy went into hiding for a reason! You'll just blow up his spot.* "He's just a guy I talked to online." *Really, Goldberg?! That's the first thing you came up with?!* "What I mean is, we emailed. About science-y stuff. Because he's an old friend of my dad's. But he moved away a long time ago. No big deal." *Please, Boob, I'm begging you to let this go.*

"Cool. Can we go to the Lair now, please?" Boob said. *Thank you! Now, forget I ever mentioned the name Butts.* "I've been watching home makeover shows with my mom and have lots of ideas about how we can spice it up. Two words: hot tub."

"Hold your horses, Bob the Builder." Rube noticed Pearl had unlocked her bike and hopped on. "Guess you're heading to chess practice, huh?"

"No, dummy. I'm coming with *you*," she replied. "Even world-class chess champions take afternoons off. But tomorrow, it's back to work.

Lala's big donation is going to do some great things. *Hopefully.* I plan to stay on top of Principal Kim to make sure the money goes where it needs to. You didn't happen to have anything to do with that, did you?"

"*Maybe*," Rube said with a twinkle in his eye. "Hey, what if I made a machine that announced your candidacy for class president?" Rube asked. "*The Declaration of Pearl*!"

"Cool your jets and commit to helping me win first. *No ghosting* this time."

"Fair enough." Rube shrugged.

"Speaking of ghosts, *Gladys is still missing*," said Boob. "We're probably still cursed!"

"Boob, *the Internet lies*! All the time. Guess what? I looked up that 'curse' last night, and there wasn't anything about it anywhere. *Nothing. Nada. Niks.* Someone left a creepy doll in the woods. That's all that happened."

"But what about all the other unexplained phenomena? I still have questions!"

"That's fine. I've got questions too. Like why do old people eat olive loaf? No one will tell me! But sometimes suspicious stuff isn't so suspicious. It's just humans doing weird stuff and not owning up to it. Trust me, there aren't any dark forces at work around here. Beechwood is just as boring as ever." *Not anymore, at least now that Professor Zeero is out of the picture.*

"We should start a band called the Slime Incident," Pearl suggested. "Obviously I'll be the lead singer, since I'm the one with the charisma *and* vocal talent."

"One thing at a time, please," said Rube.

Boob gasped. "It's officially official! We're *finally* a mystery-solving Scooby gang, complete with secret hideout and everything. I say for our second case we find the chupacabra. *Or* we could keep it local and investigate the ol' Haunted Hideaway. Whatever works best."

I've gotta throw him off the trail completely. "The Haunted Hideaway is a dead end," Rube said. "I already looked into it. And, for the record, we're *not* a mystery gang."

"Aw, you're no fun. Either way, I'm *definitely* going to need a lot of cool pants."

Well, that was easier than I thought it would be. Rube spotted Zach from across the schoolyard and waved him over. They hadn't spoken since everything went down.

"I don't know about that guy," Pearl said.

"He was proven innocent," Rube replied. "Zach isn't who you might think he is. Trust me on this."

Pearl wasn't so sure. The skeptical part of her wanted to challenge Rube, but the trusting part of her figured he saw something inside Zach that made him worth keeping around. For the moment,

that felt like enough. "Do what you've got to do," she said. "I'll meet you at the Lair."

"I'm with her," Boob said as he and Pearl took off on their bikes.

Zach sheepishly approached Rube, his eyes shifting from side to side. Embarrassed by what went down between them, he was unsure of what to say.

"What are you doing right now?" Rube asked.

"I don't know. Things are kind of crazy at the moment. My dad is being a jerk again and . . ." Zach stopped himself before saying anything further. It was clear that whatever was going on at home had him stressed. "Listen, I just want you to know that I didn't steal your machine."

"No hard feelings," Rube assured him. "You should come to the Lair. We're plotting a world takeover."

"I don't think your friends like me, though."

"They'll warm up. Bring snacks, and you'll have them eating out of your hand. *Literally*."

"Cool. I just might do that," Zach said, stifling a chuckle. "You're a good guy, Rube." He suddenly remembered something. "Ugh. I left my backpack inside. I'll have to meet you over there. The Lair is out past Stoffregen Farm, right?"

"Yep," Rube said. "How did you know?"

"Oh. Uh. I think you told me once," replied Zach. "Yeah. You definitely told me. We talked about it for sure. So, I'll, um, see you there?"

Rube gave himself a running a start and hopped on his bike. "See you there!" he yelled, riding off into the distance. "And do NOT forget those snacks!"

As Zach watched Rube go, he felt at ease. It was the first time in a long time that he'd felt so comfortable making a new friend.

A pit in his stomach kept telling him *don't mess this up*, and not just because making a new friend felt good. Zach's father put a tremendous amount of pressure on him to adapt into the school's social circles. More pressure than he let on and more than anyone else knew. Making new friends had never been easy, and moving around so much meant working hard to fit in. Being shy didn't help. But this time seemed different. Rube saw something in Zach that he didn't see in himself, and that was pretty cool. "Maybe Beechwood isn't so bad after all."

"Hey!" a voice shouted from the steps of the school. Louie Armstrong, a boy from Zach's English class, was holding up Zach's backpack. "Is this yours?"

"Yeah," Zach said, jogging over to retrieve it. "Thanks."

"I had to rummage through your bag to see who it belonged to," Louie said. "What's with that creepy doll, dude? Is that, like, a joke?"

Zach filled with fire. A bolt of raw, red rage traveled through his body like an electric current, causing him to grab the boy's arm with force. "It's not nice to go through people's private things," he growled. "Don't you dare tell *anyone* about what you saw."

Louie swung his arm away, breaking Zach's grip. "Not a problem," he said. "*Weirdo.*"

Zach looked inside his backpack to make sure nothing was out of place. All he could focus on was the pair of black eyes staring back at him.

"Thanks for everything, Gladys," he said, smiling. "I'm not done with you yet."

ACKNOWLEDGMENTS

Writing the adventures of Rube Goldberg has been a dream come true. Joyous, emotional, and surprising.

None of it would've happened without Jennifer George. Her infinite wisdom of all things Rube is unparalleled, but it was her trust that meant the most. Jennifer shared the vision from day one. You can't ask for much more than that. I'm forever grateful for her support and encouragement.

Russ Busse and I have worked together before, but this time it felt extra special. He's a sharp editor and a good guy. Over the course of making this book, he also became a father! The writing process, no matter how good it feels, can be stressful. But one chat with Russ always makes me feel better. I'm thankful he's steering this ship.

The reason you probably bought this book is because of that gorgeous Ed Steckley cover. I don't blame you. His work is beautifully expressive. His attention to detail is mesmerizing. Everything he draws has energy and life. Crafting Rube's machines is a skill, and I have no idea how Ed makes it look so effortless. We're lucky to have him.

Richard Slovak, thank you for making me look good. You're a king.

Thank you to Andrew Smith, Charlie Kochman, Jessica Gotz, Megan Carlson, Deena Fleming, Brenda Angelilli, Chelsea Hunter, Borana Greku, Gaby Paez, Hallie Patterson, Jenny Choy, Kim Lauber, Rex Ogle, Laura Nolan, Jill Smith, Bob Bookman, and Michael Bourret. Travis Kramer, your patience is appreciated. Terry and Jean Snider, you're the best parents around. Be bold!

ABOUT THE AUTHOR

Brandon T. Snider is the bestselling author of the award-winning *Dark Knight Manual*, as well as *Marvel's Avengers: Infinity War: The Cosmic Quest* series. Additionally, he's written books featuring Cartoon Network favorites like *Adventure Time* and *Regular Show*, and for pop culture icons such as Marvel's Spider-Man and Black Panther, Justice League, Star Wars, and The Muppets. Brandon lives in New York City.

ABOUT THE ILLUSTRATOR

Ed Steckley is an award-winning print and advertising illustrator. He grew up in Racine, Wisconsin, and currently lives in Queens, New York.

For more about the origins of this book's characters, please visit

abramsbooks.com/rubegoldbergmachines